I0665017

For William: patient and pushy and all those other good things.

Thank you Sherri for all of your input and fine tuning.

RISING

JAMIE VIPOND TAIT

PREFACE

They would be gone a couple of hours. That was all the time I needed.

I had packed everything I owned. I didn't have much. I threw it all in the car, while looking around at the mountain view. I wanted only to remember that – nothing else mattered. Well, except the library and the old librarian – she was different. She knew things I didn't yet understand or expect. There was no need to bother looking around the house, I couldn't care less about it. Same for the people who owned it. They were simply people I lived with.

Rocks under my feet crunched as I walked to my car and touched the door handle. A quick breeze blew up and an odd sensation came over me. Things were about to change. It was going to be very different now. My life was about to start.

I opened the door and got in, turned the key and started the engine. The radio came on and I was ready. I put the car in drive and turned onto the gravel road. The highway was only an hour away. Once there, I would be free and clear. The people who put a roof over my head wouldn't care. I was sure it would be a relief to them that I had finally left.

I looked down to the passenger seat. My map, my letter, copies of emails were all there.

It was fortunate to have known Ms. Havish. Without her, I would never have been able to escape. Although, I was sure life would have thrown me another opportunity to leave this place.

Ms. Havish was this little town's keeper of books. The town librarian. I spent my childhood and early teenage years at the library, reading and mostly hiding from beatings from the other kids. She was always very old, yet always the same. She was very different from the other townsfolk, all-knowing about many subjects. She knew things about people that others didn't. In a way she was kind of scary, but I didn't mind.

When I was younger, and the school day was over, I would make a run for the library. Most times making it there without a scratch, but those other times, the bully kids would rough me up, as ordered by their bossy leader, Jack. I could never escape him. He was the son of the people I lived with.

When I finally made it to the library, Ms. Havish would have a pile of books waiting for me to put away. She would always say, "If you're going to stay here and pester me, then you might as well make yourself useful."

I would pick up the stack and put them away. I think she pulled them out specifically for me, to distract me to keep me from bugging her. The books were about topics like vampires, magic, folklore and legends. The books about vampires were the ones I loved most. Hours passed by as I sat and read through the pages and gazed at the pictures, always wishing one day to see a real one, or go on an adventure and find one.

From time to time, Ms. Havish would sit me down, hand me a hot chocolate while she sipped her tea from an old, chipped tea cup, and tell me I should stand up to the other kids, or things that scared me. I would just shake my head no, as I was too afraid, too weak, too alone. She, of course, would laugh, and say if I put my mind to it, I could do anything I wanted to. But, she wouldn't press the issue.

When it was time to leave the safe confines of the library, I would peek my head out the door, looking around to make sure the way home was safe and free of Jack and the other kids who could ambush me. Most times, I would make it home in one piece, but there were some occasions I would arrive bloodied up. Those were usually the days Jack had nothing better to do.

Ms. Havish questioned me one day when I arrived shirt ripped, smeared, my face tear stained. She asked me. "Why didn't you ask if those kids were there?"

I wasn't sure I understood. She began to explain, in her matter-of-fact tone.

"Look out the door, and ask yourself, 'Are those brats out there?'"

Still confused I spoke up. "They aren't gonna tell me!"

She laughed at my response. "Well silly child, you're not asking *them*, you're asking *yourself*. You already know the answer. It's that simple. You may not understand it now, but one day you will. You need to learn to listen to yourself!"

She then hobbled off, leaving me a pile of books to put away.

I tried on a few occasions to do as she had suggested when leaving the library. It didn't make sense to me, but it was worth a shot. Peeking my head outside, I asked quietly.

"Are you out there?"

Never a response. How could her advice help? The other kids would sometimes still wait. I asked her again what to do, she just pointed to her head. I wished I understood what she meant.

Time passed, years actually. The kids still bullied me and occasionally beat me up. Now they were teenagers, so the punches and kicks were worse. Jack was still to blame, because he was always the instigator. One day I would get back at him, I promised.

The bullies didn't bother to chase me or wait for me when I left the library anymore. Only on my way there. So, I would still go to Ms. Havish to escape. She would, as always, leave me my pile of books to put away, still the same genre, lots of the vampire ones. She knew they were my favourite.

When I left to go home, I would play stupid little mind games to entertain myself, based on Ms. Havish's long ago suggestion of asking for answers.

"Will it be hot dogs for dinner tonight?" I laughed. "If yes, a big grey squirrel will run across the street and be chased by a black one."

This was the sign I requested for my answer. It was silly and fun. But I found myself on edge after my request was answered and the event actually happened. In other words, the grey squirrel was indeed chased by the black one across the street.

One Saturday, I sat in the library with my nose in a book. Ms. Havish limped over. She pulled out a chair and sat down with our usual drinks in hand. She looked at me, waiting for my full attention.

"So, any thoughts of what you will do with your life?" She tapped the table and waited for my reply.

I was caught off guard, usually she only made comments and gave instructions, never really asking questions.

"Uhmm, well, I suppose I could go to university or college. Or better yet, travel somewhere far away from here!"

She thought about what I said, then apparently made her mind up."How about Boston? It's a good city, it's where you should go. You're able to look after yourself well enough now. I know it will be the best place for you."

I was quiet while pondering her suggestion. Boston would be a great place to go live. It was right on the ocean, far away from here and filled with history. Salem – the witch city – was also close by. I had read all about it and wanted to go there and see it. I felt a rush of excitement. How cool it would be to see real witches, real magic. My mind started racing. If there were witches in Salem, there was bound to be vampires. I wished it was true. My body tingled.

What about money? I had a little saved up, but the library didn't pay much. I had only been working here a couple of years since graduating. I didn't have much experience under my belt to find a job somewhere else.

As if she could read my mind, Ms. Havish had an answer. "You know, an old friend of mine owns a lovely book shop. I have been speaking with him lately. He is in need of help. So I'm sure I can arrange for you to work there. Also, he can recommend suitable accommodations for you."

"Oh, that would be great." My smile turned to a frown. "I thought you wanted me to go to Boston?"

She squished up her wrinkled face. "Silly boy, it's in Boston. So now you will have a job to pay your way and you can start doing what you're destined to do." She slammed down her teacup and stood up. "I thought you were smart enough to get what I meant!" She got up and walked away.

It made sense now. But how little did I know Boston held more than a job for me.

A few weeks marched by. One windy, eventless day, I sat bored and lonely in my room wishing hard for a change. There was a tap at my door and a letter was slid under. I picked it up and quickly tore it open. Inside was my job offer from the bookshop owned by Ms. Havish's friend. Surprisingly, it paid well. I squeezed the letter tight, it was real. I would soon be out of this place. I shoved the letter in my back pocket and decided I had to go show Ms. Havish.

When I got to the library, Ms. Havish was standing at the door smiling at me. I wondered if somehow she knew I would be coming. An uneasy feeling churned in my stomach. She beckoned me inside.

She walked to the nearest table and sat down to speak. "I assume you have some news to tell me?"

"Yes! I got it. I got the job. This is great, I can't believe it." The excitement returned.

"There was never a doubt in my mind" she said, but looked to be waiting for something.

"It doesn't start for a month. That's plenty of time to get packed." The smile on my face turned into a frown and my stomach heaved at a dawning realization. "Oh man ... where am I going to live?"

Her lips smirked for a brief moment. "I have already spoken with an acquaintance of mine. She has an apartment available. It will suit you just fine."

I got up and gave Ms Havish a hug. "Thanks so much for everything."

"Someone has to watch you child." The chair scraped the floor as she rose. "Now hurry along."

"Watch me?" I laughed. My stomach felt unsettled again. I left. It was all coming together now.

During the following month I firmed up my plans, and decided to leave town without a farewell to my foster family, or anyone else, with one exception – Ms. Havish. She was the only person I would miss. The day before leaving, I stopped by the library to say goodbye. As to be expected, she was her usual self – not overly emotional, and no tears. I brought her some pink flowers. She thanked me and said that pink was her absolute favourite. After a simple good bye, she said. "Stay out of trouble." More curiously though, on my way out the door she told me, "Life is a road, pay attention to all the signs that pop up. Oh and I *will* be watching you!" With that Ms. Havish turned away. I smiled and called goodbye again to her.

I stood on the front step of the library as the door closed with a click. I knew this would be the last time I would ever see this place. I looked around and listened. I heard nothing but the wind. No bullies hiding to jump me, but I was sure, if they were in the neighbourhood, they would have. I walked down the road towards home, "If the garbage can blows over, they won't be home when I get there." I thought. The can tipped, making me smile. I would miss my little game I played on my walk home.

When I got to the house, the family who lived there including Jack were gone – I guessed out for dinner. All the better I thought. It gave me time to get my things together. I printed out directions for my long road trip and the contact information for the lady named Marge who was renting me the apartment. I still couldn't believe my luck. A good paying job and apartment in a strange new city.

It all came about so quickly and easily. Ms. Havish had this already arranged, I laughed to myself. It was as if she wanted me to go to Boston in the first place. An uneasy feeling crept through my body. It confirmed an answer to my question. I shook it off. It must be nerves.

I decided it would be best to go to bed early. I would be driving for a long time the next day, so it made sense to get more rest. I took a shower first. It would help relax me, so I could actually fall asleep.

The next morning the sun came through the little window in my room. I could hear the family moving and talking downstairs as I was starting to wake. I rolled onto my side and looked at the alarm clock – 9:30am. I had slept in longer than I thought. I sat up and looked around. This would be my last morning in this little room where I had spent years of my life. I wouldn't miss it. I stood up and stretched, yawned and walked to the bathroom across the hall.

I was in the shower when someone knocked on the bathroom door to say that they were leaving to go shopping. I sighed and relaxed. That would make it easier for me to finish getting ready and leave.

Grabbing my things from the bathroom, I brought them into my room and threw them in my bag. I dressed quickly and gathered the last of my unpacked belongings. From my closet I pulled hidden boxes of belongings. It wasn't much. With a quick last look around the room, I shut the door and headed down the stairs.

When I reached the landing I heard the doors of the van outside slam shut. The engine idled for a moment. The vehicle started to move. The gravel crunched as it drove away. They were gone.

I ran back up the stairs and grabbed my bags and as many boxes I could carry at once.

No time to waste. I wanted to get out of this place. Finally.

I opened the front door and walked outside. The dust from the gravel had settled. The coast was clear for my lone departure. The owners of the house I lived would be gone a couple of hours, unaware that was all the time I needed to get out of this place – and their lives.

CHAPTER ONE
THE END

Hours of driving and the route seemed unending. I turned up the volume on the car stereo. The windows rattled as I hit the gas and my little Honda sped down the highway. The street lights above shone onto the road and through the sunroof. I glanced into the review mirror. "Well, Markus" I smiled. "You're on your own now!"

It was the first time that I had been on my own, truly on my own. Other people I knew who had been in foster care all their lives felt alone, but this was different. I didn't have a temporary family now, just me. My hands were still shaking from the nervousness of it all. I gripped the steering wheel tighter.

I headed to my new home and adventure – Boston.

How this all happened so fast still amazed me. I knew that I would have to work and save my money to survive. But it was going to be okay. What exactly I would do or strive for, I had no clue. There was a voice in my mind that said I would be alright, my path was already laid out for me. It was either that or Ms. Havish worked some magic to put me at ease. I would never know.

I was able to pay the rent on a cheap apartment in the outskirts of Boston, thanks to my new job at a local bookstore. So supporting myself was possible, somewhat. At least I would enjoy the work. A bookstore is similar enough to a library, so I'd be right at home.

I finally arrived. The neighbourhood looked dirty and crowded, full of stone and concrete. I had never lived in a city before. The street was filled with Brownstones. My new apartment was in the one I parked my car in front of. I got out and climbed the front stairs to the main door, a pink leisure suit-clad lady was waiting for me.

"You Markus?" She asked in her thick Boston accent.

I nodded. She waved me in to follow her, and turned back inside.

After all the papers were signed and I provided the plump miserable land-lady, named Marge, with my rent cheques. I emptied the contents of my car into my new home. I only had one suitcase and three small boxes. Being a foster child, I never accumulated many belongings. Every toy, book and article of clothing were hand-me-downs passed on to me from Jack.

I looked around the empty space I now called my own. The front door opened into the kitchen. There was a little round table beside the kitchen window – one less piece of furniture I would have to buy. The other end of the kitchen opened into the main room – not that big, but there was a large bay window that looked out into the street. A view, lucky me.

The bedroom and bathroom were off the main room, both small. I looked into the mirror and laughed. My short blond hair, grey/ blue eyes and pale skin looked like it had a greenish hue. This place was filthy. I wondered when the last time the mirror was cleaned.

I started to work. This place needed to be cleaned; it should have actually been torched. But, since this was my humble abode now, I had to make the best of it. I chuckled. "Shit, this is going to take me forever!" I walked into the kitchen and began there.

The time seemed to fly. Three hours, six bottles of beer and two slices of pizza later, my work was done. The place had potential, but I was no decorator, so that wasn't likely to happen. I sat down at the little two-seater kitchen table and put my feet up. "Ahhh, peace and quiet. Just me, myself and I." That fact made me nervous. What would happen if some nut came in and murdered me? I had no relatives, my foster family was sure to be relieved I finally vacated their home and I had no friends. I was alone. Panic started to set in, again.

Trying to calm myself, I thought of something far fetched – if the crazy nut turned out to be a vampire, that would be cool. I was 6'1, 21, with short blonde hair, piercing grey-blue eyes and a swimmer's build. Now would be a *perfect* time to become immortal! If only it were that easy. I am sure a couple years of busting my ass trying to pay my way, I will have aged and look tired. So now would be a great time to capture my youth in an eternal state.

Vampires, witches, werewolves ... they all fascinated me. I always thought it would be cool to find a vampire clan and try to convince them to take me into the fold, let me be one of them. Problem was, where were they? I used to tell the other kids about my dreams of becoming an undead. It lead to having no friends and being beaten up after school because I was the weirdo kid. Oh well. At least I was away from them now.

I got up from the table and walked to my bedroom to grab the sleeping bag. Having no furniture, I might as well camp out in the living room and be able to look out the window. The bedroom had no windows. It felt like a coffin. I wanted to be a vampire and all, but I wasn't much for the coffin – was that *really* a necessity for them? When I finally meet one i'll ask. I smiled to myself again. "I'm sure a vampire would just *love* to sit down for a coffee and shoot the breeze." I could hope.

I striped my clothes off and climbed into the sleeping bag. There were a few things to do tomorrow, such as picking up food and seeing the bookstore. Excitement shot through me. I wanted to learn my route. It was good to know where I would be going. What I needed was an early start, so now would be a good time for bed.

Midnight. The witching hour.

"Imagine that." I yawned.

Suddenly I heard a series of sounds – all unrelated but happening in sequence – my watched beeped, a car door slammed, a dog barked, a bottle smashed, someone yelled and a gust of wind blew through my open window knocking over my kitchen chair. The strangest feeling came over me. It was electrifying. Something was about to happen. Change. My stomach knotted. The feeling set my teeth on edge. It was like a premonition of something bad to come. But this time I was sure it was just nerves.

The next morning the sun light streamed through the front window of my apartment. Rolling over onto my stomach, I shielded my eyes from the bright light. "Ugh. I need curtains." Still half asleep, I reached for my watch. 12 noon. "Oh, man." I sighed. So much for an early start.

Washed and dressed, Iwas set to begin my day. I hopped down the stairs to the front door of the building two steps at a time. The apartment door to the right of the main entrance flew open and a pink metallic jumpsuit stood there. Marge, the land-lady. I could see in the daylight how awful she really looked. The bright florescent lipstick seeped into the cracks around her lips, the pink blush marred her cheeks. She looked like a pink-obsessed circus clown. She glared at me. "NO JUMPING!"

I laughed at her accent and then apologised. "Sorry, won't happen again, Marge." I got to the front door and stepped into the day. Marge's door slammed. "Well, I guess I'm not one of her favourites." I thought.

Down the street I walked. I couldn't afford to maintain my car anymore, plus I lived in a big city now, so I could do without the extravagance. So I took the train. It would make sense to sell my car, because I could use the cash. I should place an ad in the paper. Make a mental note to write that down, I thought. I could be scattered brained at times, so I always need to make a list to remember things.

The train ride was slow. People got on and off. The view passed. Tunnels of dark, light of the sun, strangers, smells and sounds surrounded me. Sitting, keeping my space to myself, memories past through my head, none of them happy. I always felt alone and out of place, kind of unwanted. So my memories were of the same. Pathetic. But here I was headed out to explore Boston. It was awesome that I was here and I did it all by myself, well with Ms. Havish's help. I was on my own with no trust fund or rich parents paying my way. Just me. There was that lonely line again. "Just me." I sighed. The guy sitting beside me turned and gave me a nasty look, got up and changed seats. I felt like sticking out my tongue at him, but I would probably get beaten up. Nothing new about that, I though.

Finally, my stop. Butterflies in my stomach. Why was I so nervous? These people didn't know me, it was a new sort of adventure, my own new start at a new life. No one knew where I came from or that I was flat broke, no family, no friends. I would meet new people here and make the best of a great opportunity. I took a deep breath and got off the train.

I was at Harvard.

Harvard was bigger than I thought. But then again, I had never been to a university, so I really didn't know what to expect. I found myself in the main square, where I bought a coffee and a sandwich. Kind of pricey, but I was treating myself today, so it was ok. After wolfing down my food I decided to wander. With coffee in hand, I strolled through some stores, picked up a few little knick-knacks for my apartment, and bought a Harvard hoodie. Now I could blend in.

I found the main office of the campus and decided to look inside. The lady behind the desk was pleasant, her accent thick but different from Marge's Boston one. It was busy with students stopping in to make their inquiries. I wondered what it would be like to be able to go to a school like this. It must take a lot of money. With a last glimpse around I left.

The train ride home seemed shorter than the way there, probably because I got a feel of where I was. I went back to my apartment. With no lights on, it was dark when I opened the door. I reached to the wall and flicked the switch, the kitchen lit up. In the middle of the floor sat a cat. The fluffy feline was black as night with wide green eyes. Superstitions taught that this was a bad, very bad omen. I, on the other hand, had always believed that it was a sign of good luck. So I went with my gut. The cat looked at me, meowed, ran to the kitchen window and climbed out. I gasped. I didn't need to feel guilty about the death of a suicidal cat. But when I ran to the window, the cat was already walking away on the street below. I didn't realize that there was a fire escape outside of my kitchen. That was a relief.

I shut the window to avoid any other animal visitations and put away my new purchases.

Sitting in the kitchen again, I reviewed the list of my work duties that had been sent to me with my job information. It also included my schedule for the first two weeks. The scheduling – which was the middle of the day – didn't allow me time for much of anything. "Why couldn't my shift be different?" I put my head on the table. " Evening or morning shifts, is that too much to ask for? Errr ..." I banged my fist on the table and got up and walked in the living room. The room was only lit by the kitchen light, so onlookers couldn't see in. I stood on my toes and stretched.

I pulled off my clothes and sat on my sleeping bag that was still spread out where I left it. Might as well go to bed early. I had nothing to do, nowhere to go and no one to talk to. Tomorrow, I would start my first day at the bookstore. Hopefully there's an employee discount, because I needed a new book to read. Being in the New England area, I figured there would be all sorts of books on vampires and the occult. I didn't believe in it all, but it would be fun to read.

I closed my eyes and visualized a vampire coming into my apartment, sneaking up on me as I slept and deciding it would spare me, and make me like him ... My dreams turned violent and the vampire scratched me and thirsted to tear me into pieces, but the cat scared it away, when the paramedics arrived, the cat wouldn't let them near me. I was going to bleed to death.

I woke up covered in sweat. Usually my dreams were fun and simple, more bright, colourful and senseless. This dream was definitely a nightmare and scared me. I put my face in my hands as I sat up. Maybe that cat wasn't lucky.

I got up and went to get ready for my first day of work. Might as well be early.

It was a 20-minute train ride to the bookstore. Not bad in the grand scheme of things. The store was two storeys, and was well organized. Exposed brick walls and comfy wingback chairs were scattered here and there for patron readers. Part of my job was to make coffee and cappuccino's. I hope I got those for free. That would be a good perk. The owner, Ms. Havish's friend Dan was a nice man, white hair and beard. Well-spoken and well-educated I assumed. He explained in detail my duties, his expectations and my wages. Surprisingly, he was paying me more than I was first told. That was a bonus. It was great to be in this store. Too bad there wasn't a room for rent here. It was more like home than my apartment, plus it reminded me of the safety of the old library I had spent so much time in as a child.

I worked with one other employee, Claire. "With an E," she stated. She was a chubby brunette (clad in all black with very heavy eye liner.) and an emerald butterfly clip in her hair. She smiled at me. "Hiya! I knew you'd be coming."

I looked at her curiously, "Did you? I guess Dan told you?"

She shook her head. " No, I *saw* you coming. I see things you know. I am in touch with the spirit world. Sometimes the fairies even visit me."

She looked convinced of herself. I, on the other hand, wanted to laugh.

"So, the fairies, uhm, told you I was coming? Do they speak English?"

Claire still kept smiling, even at my doubt. "No, they come to warn me of things. I had a vision that you would come and work here and be my friend and ask me about these." She pointed at a row of books near the very back of the store under the stairs going to the second floor.

I walked over to the books and glanced at the titles. "Vampires and their Curses ...Vampires through the Ages ...Vampires and more ...Vampires for Dummies!!! That's one I haven't seen before!" Claire and I both laughed. "Claire, you had a vision about me and these books?"

She nodded. "I have to go watch the cash." she said. "You look around the store so you know where everything is. Oh, by the way, your notepad is on the floor on the second floor in isle two where the Self Help books are. You dropped it when Dan was showing you around." My mouth fell open when I checked my back pocket for my notepad. How the hell did she know that? And how did she know I was infatuated with vampires?

My watched beeped, outside a car door slammed, a dog barked, a bottle smashed, someone yelled and a gust of wind blew the store door open. The same feeling washed over me. Unsettling. It made me tense.

I walked upstairs to get my notepad and then back down to sit with Claire so she could teach me how to make coffee. We spent the rest of the work day talking about the store and Claire's visions, which she had since she was a kid. She also told me about the fairies and how they can't be sought, they find you. She considered herself very lucky to have had a couple of visitations. I thought the visits might have been thanks to some really cheap drugs, but I kept that thought to myself. I asked Claire if she had "*seen*" anymore of me and the vampire books, but she just shook her head and wouldn't say anymore about that vision. She also explained her beliefs, and how she considered herself a practicing witch. That was not a surprise.

I liked Claire. For all her strangeness and bizarre persona, she was fun. I think I might have actually made a friend.

The street lights were on, and the dark had already arrived. We closed up and Claire locked the door once we were outside. She looked at me, frowned and said. "You know, you shouldn't worry about fitting in."

I smiled. "Well, I think I'm just nervous."

She nodded and waved her hand. She bent down and picked up a fluffy black cat with large green eyes that rubbed up against her. Then Claire turned and walked away. I stared after her for a minute. I couldn't put my finger on the familiarity about it. But then I wondered how she knew I was worried about fitting in. I started to make my way home.

I stopped along the way, grabbed a burger – which I ate too fast – and reviewed the day in my head. I didn't mind my new job, it turned out better than I had thought.

I wish I didn't have to work, but it was something I had to do. I couldn't afford not to. I hoped I would sell my car soon. That would take away some stress. I hated to think about money, or I should say my lack of it. I shook my head to clear away negative thoughts. "Well, I am on to a new better life now!" I forced myself to smile and walked home.

Tonight would be a much better night for me. I had a way to entertain myself. I had a book to read. One of the many selections of the vampire books from work I had *"borrowed"* – a smirk crept across my face. I planned to return it as soon as I was done. I read fast and was careful turning pages, so it would be a good as new when I returned it. I didn't have money to waste on luxuries like books for personal entertainment.

The book was about vampires in New England. Daylighters, sightings, stories, legends, how to find ...*the window slid open and the shadow crept in. The dark form made its way towards the young man asleep on the floor. The shadow seemed to smell the air or breath something in. It was impossible to tell. It dragged its razor sharp nails gently across the victims bare back. It struck at its victim, violently slashing, blood splattered ...*

"OH MY GOD ..." I gasped and gulped for air. "Oh, holy ..."

What was with this dream? I sat up quickly panicked. I must have thrown my sleeping bag off during the night. I was almost naked dripping with sweat. I think I might need to start sleeping in the bedroom. Maybe having a open window nearby is creeping me out. Must be what is scaring me. I never before had, so many nightmares. Or maybe I am on edge. "Oh, who knows." I lay back down to catch my breath.

I rolled over onto my stomach and groped for my new book. I didn't have to go to work for a few more hours, so I might as well read and take advantage of my spare time. "Chapter three, Vampires of Daylight ..." I had read a little about their powers of tolerance to the sun, but this book might contain something new. Maybe New England vampires have some different powers or talismans to withstand the light. I *wish* I could meet a day vampire. That would be awesome. If only ... My body started to tingle a little, maybe from excitement.

After hours of reading, I showered and headed to work. Since it was a windy and unseasonably cool today, I decided to walk. I still had time to get there by foot, and it was cool enough so I wouldn't be sweaty. I could use the exercise. Back home, I walked all the time and, in a way, I missed it. Home? Well, not so much missing the place where I lived, but I missed my habits: The woods I cut through on my walk to school; the park I sat on the swings and just daydreamed; the ledge where I used to sit and read that had a view of the town below. It was dangerous to climb up that hill, but I like the peace. And I missed the library. A soft sigh escaped my lips.

I arrived at work without realizing it. I was so into my thoughts and memories, I hadn't noticed. Considering it was my second time there, it was strange I already knew my way.

Claire was there. Once again, emerald butterflies hung in her hair. They made her hair look like a Venus fly trap that ensnared its prey. I laughed to myself.

Claire waved at me. "Hello Markus! Dream well?"

I thought of my nightmare. "Yah, I slept alright. You?" I started to pour myself a coffee while she appeared to consider her response.

"Well..." she started, "I dreamt well, the fairies said you ...well, you cried out in pain."

I put the pot of coffee back on the burner and said nothing for a moment. It was my turn to consider my response. "I did have a bad dream last night, but I sure didn't cry our in pain." I looked at Claire wondering what she was thinking, wondering what the fairies had told her.

She smiled. "Okay." She had such a thoughtless look to her. I didn't notice yesterday, but she *did* come across like she was a few brain cells short. But, she was still a nice person.

"Do you think it will be busy today?" I posed the question as a distraction. "Actually, does it ever get really busy?"

Claire started to wipe the front counter. "Oh, no. It hardly gets busy. That's what's so perfect about this place. You can get your personal things done *and* look after your duties here. I love it." She made larger circles with the cloth.

That certainly was a perk. "Thanks for telling me." I grinned.

"Plus, we have all this coffee. It would be a shame to waste it." We both laughed.

The remainder of the daylight hours were spent with Claire revealing to me her secrets about maintaining the store, serving the customers and getting all of her work done. It seemed she had it all worked out. She was happy and I was thankful for her tips about balancing it all.

The street lights came on and the sun set. There was still an hour before closing, so it was quiet. There were no customers. Claire was on the second floor putting stock away. The bell rang as the front door opened.

A man walked in. He had short black hair and a trimmed goatee. He was the same height as me, tanned but pale. He looked roughly my age. He smiled at me and walked past the front counter and down one of the isles into the store.

Only a second later, the man emerged from the isle with a book in hand.

I smiled. "Hi. How are you tonight?"

He smiled back. "I am very well. Thank you for asking. And how are you this good evening?" He lowered his head slightly but looked up at me with his eyes. There was a strange look to them. Almost ... inviting.

My stomach knotted as I fumbled with his book and typed the price into the cash register. " I'm good thanks. Is this all?" I slipped the book into a bag.

He smile broadened as he nodded. "Book-wise, yes. That is all." His eyes pierced through me. But they wandered back to the register, then quickly to the street as someone walked by the storefront window.

He paid with cash, said good night and left the store.

He was friendly enough, but I still felt there was something odd about the look he gave me. My mind flashed to different ideas about what it meant. But I let it rest at him being very polite, proper and upper-crust. I'm sure a lot of people here will be similar. Good breeding, I suppose.

We closed up and Claire and I parted ways. It was another good day at work.

The rest of the week went off without a hitch – also, no more nightmares. They must have been stress related. Dan, the bookstore owner, was more than accommodating and adjusted my shifts for me. I even managed to sell my car. I was more happy now than I have ever been.

CHAPTER TWO

SECRET

The sun hadn't even started to rise when I woke up. I was so nervous and I didn't know why. I tried to fall back to sleep, but just tossed and turned, there was no hope. Instead, I grabbed a book and read.

Hours later I got up. Might as well start my day.

I poured some cereal and sat at my kitchen table looking out the window. My new friend, the black cat, whom I named Whiskers (because it was the first name I thought of) slept curled in a ball on the fire escape landing. It was the first time I had my own pet. Well, he wasn't really mine, but I pretended anyway. Besides, it was nice to have some sort of company. I finished my breakfast and got up to put the bowl in the sink. A big yawn escaped me and I stretched. Whiskers looked up at me, then went back to his nap.

I showered. Uneasiness had overtaken me. It was as if I was going on a date. Butterflies swirled in my stomach. I even had a hard time picking out my clothes. My choice in the end was my new Harvard hoodie. I stepped out of my apartment, locked the door and walked down the stairs to the street.

The train was packed, standing room only, but that was to be expected on a weekday. I wasn't a fan of crowds. I liked my personal space and I was always uncomfortable when others got too close. It made my skin crawl.

The train doors opened. I followed the crowd out and onto the bright sunny street. With my hands in my pocket I strolled at a slow pace into Harvard Square. There was plenty of time to kill before work started and I decided to spend it here. I grabbed a coffee. After a second thought, I bought two. The first one I would guzzle, the second one I would savour. Others around me had the same idea. I looked closer at the other coffee drinkers as we sat in the tree filled courtyard with metal grid worktables and chairs outside the coffee shop.

Everyone's faces showed signs of sleep deprivation and anxiety. I wondered for a moment whether my own face looked the same. I thought about it for a little longer, the answer never came. A red sports car drove past and down the street. A chill crept up my back, giving me a sense of foreboding.

I sipped at my coffee and gazed at the blue, afternoon sky. A perfect day weather-wise, that always made me feel good. Hopefully that was a good omen. I crossed my fingers just in case. I wished I would get a sign that this were true. Maybe a bird would come and land on my table where I sat alone, that would be my sign. I smiled.

Since moving to the city, I hadn't asked for signs. But now it felt like the right thing to do. From now on, before every decision or situation I wanted to know about, I would. I'd secretly asked for a particular occurrence to happen so that I would be certain of the answer. I knew it was strange to do, but why stop now?

Maybe the need for premonitions was a need the reassurance.

I smiled thinking about Claire and her visions of events to come. Maybe I needed butterflies in my hair to act as antenna to fine tune predictions. That would be a sight.

A bird flew down and perched itself at my table. It bobbed its head around, chirped and looked right at me. I stared back. It flew into the tree it came from.

"Well, I guess that answered my question!" I said to myself. My day was going to be good. I sipped my coffee. Was it just luck? Coincidence? I looked around to see if the strangers had noticed. I supposed that no one was privy to the conversation I was having in my head, so it wasn't likely that they were holding their breathe waiting for the bird to land where I asked it to. I could be such a loser at times.

I got up and walked towards the school grounds. Students were moving in all directions. There was no pattern or line of people to follow. They all scattered to the four winds.

I took the last swig of my coffee and ditched the cup in a nearby garbage can. I turned and walked around the side of a building, past a set of doors. As I did, the door swung open and hit me hard, pushing me back.

I was a little shocked – and a little pissed. People should watch where they're going. The blonde girl who had forced her way out the door looked back at me. She curled her lip up at me like I was some homeless beggar, who had just harassed her for change. Her bright red sweater was a little small.

My mood darkened. The stupid blonde bimbo tainted my enjoyment of this area. Angry, I changed direction and headed back towards the train station. I dug into my bag and pulled out an apple trying to comfort myself with food.

The train arrived at my stop. I exited. A few people got off here, so it didn't feel like I was being thrown or hurried from the doors this time. I went straight to the bookstore to start my shift. Early.

Claire was standing at the front counter – actually she was leaning on the front counter, engrossed in some large book that lay open in front of her. She looked up when the little bell rang as I opened the door.

"Hiyah Markus!" She smiled. "How was your day? I just *know* that things are working out for you. A little birdie told me so!" She gave me a grin and raised an eyebrow.

"Oh?" I said. "Well, yah, it wasn't all that bad." I laid my knapsack down on the floor behind the front counter. " I'm starving. Is it okay if I pop over to the sandwich place across the street and grab something?"

Claire slid something wrapped in foil on the counter towards me.

"Here." She scrunched her nose. "You can have this. I bought it 15 minutes ago. It had a slice of meat on it! I don't eat animals."

I should have figured, I thought to myself and chuckled.

I unwrapped the sandwich, which consisted of an assortment of veggies and a few slices of what looked like turkey. "Awesome! Thanks Claire." I took a bite. It tasted good.

"So, why don't you eat meat? You don't like it? Is it a fairy thing? Does it bug them?" That might have been a little cruel, but I couldn't resist.

"No. Duh. I'm a vegetarian."

"So, do the fairies eat meat?" I took another bite of the sandwich.

"No, they eat plants, woodland berries and vegetables, mostly water works for them. I suppose acorns and ....". Her voice trailed off as the front bell jingled.

A cool evening breeze swept past me as a familiar man walked in.

It was him again. The short black hair, goatee, the same inviting smile and eyes that saw right into my soul. I stared for a moment too long. Claire elbowed me in the ribs.

"Markus? Whoo hoo? You okay?"

"Oh. Uhmm, sorry. I zoned out for a moment." I glanced around and noticed the guy was already out of sight and must be mulling around somewhere in the store.

She looked at me and smiled like she *knew* something I didn't know.

"I think he likes you! I think he has the HOTS for you!" Claire giggled.

"Whatever Claire! Did the fairies tell you that? Hmm?"

"No, but I have a feeling you'll be seeing more of him than you know." A strange annoyed look flickered across her face, then disappeared.

I rolled my eyes and laughed at her. She smiled in her usual thoughtless way.

I finished my sandwich and thanked her for the free meal. She absolutely refused money for it. Claire turned and walked away picking up a stack of magazines from the end of the long front counter. I already forgot I was here to work and I really should have put the stock away. But because she had already had that taken care of, I got out my book and began to read.

Moments later I was too engrossed in my book to notice a figure standing at the front counter.

"Pardon me?" The strangely calming voice interrupted. "Are you enjoying school?"

"What?" I looked up. "I'm sorry I didn't catch that?"

It was the tall black haired man who was in front of me now.

"Are you enjoying school?" He asked again. His expression serious.

My heart skipped a beat. There was definitely something different about him, something out of the ordinary, but I just couldn't place it.

"Uhmm ... Yes, I am." I took a breath, fumbling my words. "Ar ...Are you?"

"Well, to answer your question, yes." He pointed a finger at me.

"I assume you attend Harvard? I do as well. The hoodie you are wearing is a definite give away. Who could miss the large print?" He laughed. It was a distinct ha, ha, ha. I felt very insignificant compared to him.

I looked down and glanced at the school name written across my chest. "Oh. Yeah, I guess that would do it. Stupid me!" I looked at him again, my palms were starting to sweat.

"A shame I didn't see you there today." He placed his book on the counter and pushed it toward me. "Perhaps tomorrow."

Anxiously, I looked down at the book, then clued in to the fact that he wanted to purchase it. Because I worked here, it was my job to ring it in for him, not to stand there like an idiot.

He stuck his hand out to shake mine. "I'm Darren Von Land, and you are?"

A little surprised at this, I answered. "I'm Markus Benson. Nice to meet you."

"Well, Markus Benson, it is nice to meet you as well. I am *sure* I will be seeing you again."

He dropped the cash on the counter and picked up his book. His eyes looked into me again. It was like I could feel static.

"I hope so." I said. "I mean, uh, after class is there anywhere good to go for a drink or eat?" I stood still, hoping he didn't catch what I had said.

He smirked. "There is a pub across the street from the school. I am sure anyone can point the way for you."

"Oh. Right. Well, maybe I will check it out tomorrow evening then. You know, after class ends."

Darren smiled. "Have a good evening Marcus. Until later." He turned towards the door and waved as he exited.

"See yah!" I called. My eyes followed him as he went. But I was distracted by a black, thick furred cat tapping its paws on the store window as it stretched.

The door closed and Claire reappeared. She was humming to herself. She came around to the back of the counter and started to rummage through some drawers until she found what she was looking for, then left again. I went back to my book and tried to continue reading.

The next day I had off from work. I was stressed. My mind kept replaying last night's meeting with Darren. I should have told him that I didn't go to school. Now he would think I was like him and all those other wealthy kids. I didn't go to Harvard. What was I going to do?

I would fake it. If I saw Darren at the pub tonight, we could hang out for a bit. We could become friends and then I could tell him the truth. It would all be cool. Claire was my one and only friend and I didn't want to risk losing Darren as a potential.

It was evening as I sat down on a bench in Harvard Square. Not as many people as earlier, but still enough. My stomach growled. I reached down into my knapsack to find my apple, but I couldn't feel it. I looked inside. "Ah hah! There you are!" I pulled the apple out.

Startled, I jumped a little. Darren Von Land sat to my immediate right. I was certain no one was here a moment ago.

He looked at me and smiled. "Is it a regular occurrence for you to converse with your food? Very entertaining, please don't stop on my account." He laughed and his brown eyes were shining.

"Uhmm. Sometimes." I smiled. "It never seems to answer back though." I shifted to face him.

"I see." Darren replied. "I should make a note of that. Actually,

I'm here to study how students interact with their fruit in times of stress and boredom."

I had to laugh. "Sounds like that'd be entertaining!"

Darren and I sat for a while longer talking. When you got past his haughty use of language, he was a really good guy. He had a good sense of humour and was very intelligent.

We somehow got onto the topic of premonitions. I don't know why, but I felt compelled or free to tell him secrets I kept to myself. I told him about Claire and her Fairies. Also, I told him about how I asked for "signs" of things I wanted to happen. Darren looked like he found it amusing. I'm not sure he believed a word of it.

We got up and walked a little. The street lights and lamps were on. Darren turned to me. "Well Markus, I have to say it was good to have someone to talk to, who isn't full of themselves." He smiled and his eyes looked into me again. It felt like he could see in my mind making me feel embarrassed.

"No problem. I may not have the looks, clothes, money or brains like some people, but I can communicate with fruits and vegetables." I bit my lip, hopping he didn't think I was a freak.

"That you can indeed!" He grinned. " Did you want to get a coffee or beer?"

"Uhmm, sure. Sounds good. Where ?"

Darren turned and pointed across the street. "That's the pub I had mentioned. Hopefully, we can find a seat. It is usually quite busy. It would be nice if it was a little quieter for once."

I laughed. "Let me ask for a sign to see if we will find a quiet spot in there. Uhmm, how about ..." I looked around. "There!" I pointed, excitement shooting through me. " See the guy walking with the box. If he trips, drops the box and falls face first into the lap of the woman at that table – then our answer will be a yes!"

Darren raised his eyebrow, but said nothing.

We watched as the man carried his box.

He suddenly tripped. His foot must have caught the uneven sidewalk. In an effort to catch his balance, he ended up thrusting the box forward. It shot out of his hands and fell to the ground. The man was hopeless, he fell – he ended up on his hands and knees on the ground, his face planted in a woman's lap, who had been sitting quietly enjoying her warm beverage on the patio.

Darren's jaw dropped. "But how?"

"You know, just my special power!" I smirked. " Come on, let's go get our seat since we *know* it will be there."

Darren regained himself, but there was still a questioning look on his face. We crossed the street to the pub, finding it was very quiet. We sat down at a table by the window that was further removed from the rest.

Darren stared at me. "You weren't kidding were you? About making things happen?"

"Nope. But it doesn't work all the time." I shrugged.

He clasped his hands together on the table. "It is very strange you know, not so much of a premonition as it is *willing* something to happen. That could be a very dangerous gift Markus." His face became serious.

I looked out the window. "I suppose it could be, but I never thought of it as a gift. It's a fun way to see if the things I want to happen actually will. It's really more coincidence than anything else."

"I think you should be very smart with this gift. Be careful of what you ask for – or *will* to happen – you don't want something bad to happen ... But I *suppose*...you could ask for something ... rewarding." He leaned back in his chair and smiled deviously.

My body felt flushed. I shifted in my seat. "Darren, it's not a gift. It's a little game I've played since I was a kid." I said. "It's not like I can look out this window and say, *a red car will speed down here and smack into the lamp post over there and the driver will be ejected through the wind shield.*" What a stupid thing to say. I was irritated at myself now. My body tingled as I thought about my awful example.

I folded my arms across my chest. Clearly, I was sulky and miserable now. For sure Darren would think I was childish. Considering we were just starting to become friends, I was surprised that he didn't get up and tell me to grow up, fuck off and leave. If I acted like this with people I had just met, I would always be alone.

Instead, Darren leaned forward and clasped his hand together on the table. Very smooth hands I noticed, everything about him was smooth. He was almost perfect. The rich could afford to do things to their bodies to make themselves perfection, I thought.

Darren smiled and spoke. "I am sorry Markus. I suppose I find your gift – sorry, your *signs* – very interesting and yet unnerving. I have never come across anything like it before. It could be premonition mixed with willingness. A bending of prophecies to your own will ..." He sat in thought for a moment.

I shook my head. "I should apologise. I didn't mean to be pissy, but I thought maybe you were making fun of me a little. People generally aren't nice to me for some reason. You're the first person I have ever told what I can do. I don't even know *why* I told you ..." But inside I felt like I had the need to pour my thoughts to him. Truth serum maybe? Did that even exist?

He looked at me with appraising eyes. "I don't understand why others would not like you, you are quite handsome." He grinned. "AND entertaining. But to answer your question, people, for *some* reason, always tell me their dark secrets and share themselves with me. I suppose that is my ... how did you call it? Special power."

A horn honked outside. It drew our attention to the window. A small red sports car sped dangerously down the street. Suddenly it swerved. The car jumped the curb and smacked into a lamp post. The sheer force of impact made the metal wrap around the pole. The driver's body ejected through the front windshield. It hit the ground and rolled leaving bloody marks. Finally pooling around the crumpled body.

"OH MY GOD!" I yelled as I stood up.

Darren inhaled sharply.

I turned away from the window and yelled for someone to call 911.

I looked back again, toward the gruesome scene. "What have I done? Oh my god, what have I done?" I knew I had caused this.

I fell into my chair. I could see a crowd of people surrounding the body that lay on the ground. My body started to shake with fright at the realization of what I had just done. Nausea overtook me. I cupped my face with my hands.

Darren *was* right.

Darren *warned* me.

Darren *was* gone.

I don't know how, or when, I got home. My dreams that night were frightening. The shadow creature that tore at me was more violent, as though I embodied everything it hated. I must be utterly destroyed.

When I woke, I was soaked. The covers long thrown off in the night, and I lay naked shivering from fear, fright, and realization of what happened the night before. Then the cold touched my sweaty body.

I lay there longer. Replaying everything in my mind again. I felt drained. I hated myself. For the first time in my life, I wanted to die, not to prove myself as a successful person. I couldn't stand the guilt of causing someone to die with my childish game. I began to shudder and cry.

For days I was holed up in my dark windowless bedroom. I hadn't gotten up, hadn't eaten. I cradled myself at moments. I hit myself. I cried and sobbed. That was all I was capable of.

I was barely aware of the lock turning at my front door. Barely aware of pink clad Marge's voice, miserable, speaking to someone. "Have him shut up, I can't take it anymooore or he's outta here. This is so retawwded!"

A man's voice thanked her.

The door closed. Two sets of feet were walking into my apartment. Still half aware, half crazy, I thought it was the shadow finally here to kill me.

A girl's voice. Sweet and simple, called my name. "Markus? Markus? They *TOLD* me he was here!"

The doorknob to my dark room turned. Darren's voice called in. "Markus? Hey are you alright? Claire, he's in here. Just wait there, he might want to cover up a bit before female company."

"Okay," her usual response.

Darren shut my bedroom door and turned on the light. He walked toward where I lay and looked down at me. "Well, you're lucky I am such a nice guy that I won't take advantage of this situation." He smirked and gave my naked body a once over. "Alright Markus, you have to pull yourself together. Let's go, up, up!"

With no effort at all, he picked me up. He cradled me in his arms like a parent holds their delicate child, his cold skin felt soothing against my ragged body. He carried me into the bathroom and sat me gently in the tub. "Okay, here we go."

He turned the shower on full blast. Cold water shot at me, making my body go into momentary shock. The all over cold awoke me from my state.

I looked at Darren stunned, now fully aware of my strange situation. I was laying in my bathtub, water spraying at me, and there was Darren, perfectly pulled together, smiling at me, clearly enjoying himself at my expense. I felt a little uncomfortable. Actually, I felt more stupid than anything.

Darren had left me alone to take a proper shower. It felt good to be clean, almost like I was washing away the horror that put me in shock. Maybe the fact that the only two people I knew – and who were the closest to friends I had – were here to help me, made me feel a little better.

I dried off and was about to go to my room when the bathroom door opened. Darren poked his head in. "Hey. Here you go." He handed me a pile of clothes. "I don't want you in that room again, not until it has been aired out and cleaned at least. So I took the liberty of finding you something decent to wear."

"Thanks. I'll be out in a minute."

"Don't keep us waiting long." He smiled at me.

"Okay. I won't. Now do you mind?" I grinned at him as I pushed the door closed on him and his roaming eyes.

He picked out a fitted grey sweat shirt and blue jeans.

I noticed it was dark out when I walked past the front room windows. Claire and Darren sat at my kitchen table. Claire had my adopted black cat on her lap. She was petting it and talking to it in a sweet whiney voice. I walked into the kitchen, leaned against the counter and looked at the pair. "Thanks for coming to check on me guys! I'm sorry I got all weird." I was embarrassed.

Claire smiled. "I knew you needed help, they told me. Your cat told them." She looked down at the feline in her lap. "Isn't that right cutie? Ohhhh sweetie kitty!"

Darren rolled his eyes and laughed.

I looked at him. "Thanks! I owe you."

He held his hand up. "Don't worry about it Markus. I have been around people who have gone through similar situations. No need to thank me. But on second thought, you can still owe me. I might eventually want a favour." He put on a very angelic face and smiled.

I gulped.

I took in a breath. "So, I guess the driver was dead when the ambulance got there?" I didn't want to hear the answer, but I knew I had to. I needed to get it over with. It was odd I was fully functioning and clear to process my thoughts after being so clouded only an hour before.

Claire took her attention from the cat and looked at me. "Nope. I heard on the news the guy was just scratched up! The police were chasing him because he hit some girl. Hit and run you know. She's alive, but broken legs and stuff. Anyways, they chased him and they lost him, so he would have gotten away. But by some miracle he hit the lamppost and totalled his car. He was so drunk that he was just scraped up. If he wasn't so inebriated he'd probably be dead, squashed and smushed! The police nabbed him. Happy ending!" She smiled. I don't think she took a single breath when she told the story.

Darren now spoke. "I called the police after we watched it happen, but when I got back to our table you were gone. I was a little worried. Especially after our *conversation.*" He emphasize the word. "So I went looking for you. I ended up going home as it got too late. When I stopped in the bookshop and you hadn't shown up for a couple of days I was really worried. Claire was the one who told me you hadn't been in and her friends the ... fairies is it?" Claire nodded. "The fairies told her that your cat said you were in a very bad way. So, here we are, come to save you." He grinned at me. I knew he was secretly laughing at Claire.

I hadn't known until just now, how reassuring it was to have people actually worry about me, and actually want to help. I was lucky to have met these two completely different people. It would be good to have them in my life.

We talked for a little while longer. Eventually Claire had to go.

"See you Markus! Be well, I covered for you at work, so whenever you feel like coming back, you can! The fairies said you would help me out when I needed it in the future." She waved both hands goodbye and went out the door.

Darren stood still in my kitchen, he seemed to be searching for words. "Markus? I know we talked about your *signs* ... It seems I was wrong. When you asked for something, or said something would happen, it created something good." He thought for another moment. "You remember the guy who tripped? The one with the box?"

I nodded. He continued. "Well, I have seen him with the woman he fell on.

They now meet at the coffee shop every night, looks like they are kind of a couple, considering they are always touching and kissing each other. It looks like your little gift helps fate maybe, in a good way."

I listened to what he said. I wasn't so sure he was right. "Darren, that sounds good and all, but that night I found out that I can apparently make *real* things happen, just by willing it to be. Maybe it was coincidence, maybe luck. But I don't think it is *always* a good thing. I wish it was so. But I don't believe it. If I *can* do these freaky things, then I really should be more careful, just like you tried to tell me. I honestly don't think I have some special gift to make things happen. Maybe, just maybe, I can predict something. Anyway, I am not some saint who makes the world a better place. That guy still got hurt."

"I think it *is* a gift Markus." Darren walked towards me. "You are special. If you don't believe me, well ..." He shrugged his shoulders.

"I don't know, isn't it a little too weird?" I looked at him, not able to see much as the room was too dark. "If it was Claire telling me about this, I would maybe believe, because with her you never know. She's kind of kooky anyway. But this is *me* we're talking about. Nothing special here!"

He walked closer to me. "Try it again. Go on Markus do it. See what you can manage. I don't think in my whole life I have met someone like you – not weird, but special. Magical almost."

Magical, the word made my stomach turn to butterflies.

"Okay, *if* I have some special gift ..." I looked around I couldn't see anything, except for the light coming from the kitchen. Beside the light was the emergency sprinkler system. My tone became matter-of-fact. "If I have this gift as you call it, then the sprinklers will go off right now!"

I looked back into the kitchen and nothing happened.

"See! Nothing." I said angrily, my body tingling.

"I think you're wrong Markus." Darren stood his ground.

We stood there for a moment.

Then without warning, the ceiling burst into a rain storm. The cold water started to shower down on us. It went everywhere. I stood there, amazed. Maybe I was special after all. Then fear of what this could mean started to set in.

Darren froze, his face hard. The water dripped in his ears. He was barely holding back his anger. "Do you believe me now? Hmm?" Water continued to pour down onto him. "Well, if you do, would you *please* ask for the sprinklers to shut off, because I am soaked and I still have to get home you know!" He ran his hand across his head, forcing the water off his short glistening black hair. He muttered something inaudible.

CHAPTER THREE

WICKED

I sat on the floor with my legs crossed. Darren was frustrated. "Come on Markus, con-cen-trate! If you want to work on controlling this, you have to practise, practise, practise!"

"Easy for you to say! I am the one who has to do all the work you know." I was feeling tired and it was showing in my biting tone. "I want to rest. We've been practising every bloody night. Can't we go for a beer? You know, go out and have a little fun or something? PLEASE?" I was pleading now.

He looked at me, his smooth tan face softened. It was odd that there never seemed to be any creases, no bags under his eyes from lack of sleep like mine. No signs of stress or wear. Good genetics I supposed – or Botox – or something else.

He sat down on the floor beside me. "Okay, we stop. I just want to help you. I don't want to see you fall into a slump again. I don't think you could handle another incident."

His cold hand slapped me hard on the back. "Really, I would like to forgo having to pick your sweaty naked carcass off the floor for a second time!" He barked.

I raised my eye brow and grinned. "Really? And here I thought I was giving you a nice treat. People never appreciate the things I do for them."

In the weeks that past since the night he and Claire had come to rescue me, Darren and I had become best friends. He had figured out that I didn't go to Harvard. I realized there were things about him that were obvious, but never stated. But that was fine. I enjoyed his company, and he mine. He helped me practise using my gift. Actually, I practised how to not use it.

Darren suggested that I think of it like a sensation. If I felt that sensation, then things will happen, but if I can stop the sensation, then the 'magic,' for lack of a better word did not occur. It was a theory of his, but I had to admit it worked. I guess that was the tingle I had always felt.

It seemed that after the night of the accident, floodgates opened and things were happening all around me. On a sunny afternoon, I was bored and feeling more lonely than usual. I wished Darren would show up. When he did, he put his foot down, and that is how we began the control lessons. For the first time, he was angry. He was forced against his will to visit me mid-day. He was uncomfortable, flushed and sweating. Weird, considering he was always Mr. Icebox. Anyway, I guess he was irritated by having to leave in the middle of class. He took his studies seriously. I had never seen him during the day except this one occasion. He was taking every class possible.

So here we were, weeks later. I needed a break. Even just for one night, I would do anything for something different.

"Alright Markus. What would you like to do? Where would you like to go?"

Laying on the floor, he leaned back on his elbows, his shirt rose a little above his stomach. It was impossible to not notice his chiselled abdomen.

"Geez, I guess you never eat to get a stomach like that. I should try that! I do sit ups everyday and all I can manage is a six pack, what do you have Darren, a 24?" I padded my own stomach. I felt fat compared to him, but that wasn't the case at all.

"Well, Markus, It's the strict liquid-only diet. It makes all the difference. I figure I have to look good or you wouldn't be my friend." He smiled.

"Whatever!"

He sat up turned and stared me in the face. I looked away, nervous about the intensity in his eyes. He lowered his head but then stood up. "Alright, grab your coat, let's get going." He left the room and walked into the kitchen. I felt sorry for him, he was always on good behaviour, and tried hard to be a good friend. I seemed to always make comments, or say something that upsets him. It was my stupid attempt at humour.

I got up and walked to where he was waiting. I grabbed my coat from the back of the chair and my keys from the counter. "Let's hit the road." Smiling, I put my arm around his cold hard shoulders. "We need to get drunk!" His stiff posture soften as he shrugged.

We walked down the streets in search of a pub. In Boston there were many to choose from. Finally, Darren led the way to one that seemed to be almost empty and very quiet.

"You like quiet places don't you?" I remarked.

He looked at me. "What do you mean?"

"Well, you always manage to find places, or want us to go places that are uninhabited. Just an observation."

"You're right. I suppose it is force of habit. Habits are very difficult to break you know." He walked up the steps and opened the heavy door. Holding it open, he waved me to enter, offering no further explanation.

"Thanks. You're such a gentleman Darren." I grinned, walking into the pub.

"I suppose I am." He smirked.

I walked towards a table near the window, my own habit. "You know, since you're a gentleman and all, it is only right that you pay for the drinks. It's the gentlemanly thing to do." I flashed a devious smile at him.

He took his coat off and hung it on the back of his chair. "I unfortunately must agree, that *is* the proper thing to do. Next time I suppose you can play the part of the gentleman?"

"Me? I'm just a penniless hick, I can't afford these fancy places." I motioned around the pub. It was hardly fancy. Actually, it was a hole. "I would have to sell all my worldly belongings and my body to just afford a small meal here." I put my coat over my head to look like a nun or a beggar.

Darren finally laughed. "You really crack me up, Markus. Truly, you do."

"Don't laugh too much" I warned. "It would take years of Botox to erase the laugh lines."

"Well, I certainly would not want to waste my fortune on that."

I smiled. "You could always find a vampire, ask him ever so politely – as you always do – to bite you. Then you wouldn't have to worry about wrinkles ever!" I cracked myself up.

Darren laughed a little, but not enough to be convincing. I guess my last joke wasn't that funny.

I took a swig of beer, nice and cold. Darren was halfway through his pint. I was too busy laughing to have seen him drink.

Vampires, I thought to myself. I almost forgot I still had a book on them that I borrowed from work. Not the same one when I started, but this one was about vampire legends and myths, almost like prophecies. It was interesting. *Interesting* ... I never thought to use my new gift like that. "You know what Darren? I never considered the possibility that I could ask to see a real vampire?"

Darren looked horror struck. "NO! Don't do something STUPID like that. You could end up bringing a monster that could hurt people. Is that what you want? Really? " He was very angry, I could see his tanned hands turn white as he squeezed them into fists.

I could feel the odd sensation building in me, like it was about to grant my wish. Concentrating hard I extinguished it immediately. He had a good point. "Sorry. I didn't think ..."

He was still tense. "No. Obviously you didn't think. Try not to be stupid and get people hurt. Why do you think I have been pushing you to control this?" He pointed to his head.

"Okay. I get it. I won't consider things like that. Just take a chill pill Darren. I get what you're saying."

He looked very angry still, but did not say another word.

We sat in silence.

Looking out the window I drank my beer. Why was Darren was so mad? I got his point and all, but I wouldn't cause something stupid to happen. Maybe he was scared of vampires or he had nightmares when he was a kid or something. In any case, I got it. I knew what he meant, and I wouldn't '*magic*' some disaster into being.

Yet, I *suppose*, if I thought it out carefully and was *very* specific, then maybe I would be able to get what I wanted and make sure no one got hurt. Hmm. That idea definitely had merit. I didn't think it wise to share my thoughts with Darren about this. He still looked like he would rip my head off if I even mentioned vampires again.

I put away these vampire thoughts for later, when I could think it through, when I was totally sober. After a pint beer or two I was sure I would end up goofing something up.

"Darren?" I waved my hand in front of his face. "You okay? You still mad?"

"No." He sighed. "I'm not. I'm just frustrated, that's all. My apologies. I didn't mean to yell." He looked down at his hands as he folded them into his lap. "I just don't want to see something awful happen to you."

I lifted my beer. "Well, then, I accept your apology, so you can buy me another one. And don't worry, nothing bad is going to happen!"

"You *do* realize you have to work early tomorrow Markus? Sporting a hangover isn't always the most appropriate. But, if you insist." He caught the waitress's attention and pointed to his empty glass. She nodded. He turned back to me "You're not going to get too drunk are you?"

"Who *me*?" I feigned shock. "Never!" I faked a southern accent. "Us country boys can out-drink you city folks any time!" I smiled widely and finished what was left in my glass.

Darren rolled his eyes at me. He knew full well I had a limited tolerance to beer, after two pints I would be shit-faced.

The waitress brought us a couple more rounds. We talked and laughed. Actually, I slurred my words more than talked. Clearly, I was heavily intoxicated. Darren, of course, laughed at my expense.

Morning came quickly and my head throbbed. The pounding was unbearable to say the least. I turned onto my side, my bed bounced. "Uh, man." Was about all I could get out of my mouth. I reached for the bedside table and felt for the lamp switch and flicked it on.

A big glass of water and two pills stared at me. "Someone was thinking of me." I took them and drank the water. It felt a little better, but was still so thirsty, my stomach felt tight and knotted. Was I sick last night? I couldn't remember. The last thing I recalled was fumbling with my keys at the front door.

I swung my legs over the bed and slowly forced myself to stand.

The lamp light wasn't too painful on my eyes. I wondered what time it was. It was hard to tell the time of day in my room because it had no windows and I always slept with the door closed. I walked towards the door, grabbed the handle and opened it up.

The bright sunlight hit me like a freight train. Instantly, my head pounded harder. "Ughh, come on." I whined, dragging my feet to the kitchen while keeping my hand in front of my eyes to block the sun.

I went to the sink and drank water until is swished in my stomach. I noticed the time. Noon. "Fuh-uhk!" I was late for work.

I showered, tried to eat some dry toast then headed to work. Money was tight. I absolutely could not miss a day, even though it would be painful.

The bell of the store's front door jingled as I pushed it open. Claire wasn't at the front counter so I glanced around. I walked behind the counter and threw my coat over a stool.

It was while I was pouring myself a cup of coffee that I heard Claire's heavy footsteps coming down the stairs from the second floor.

"Hey Claire. How's it going?" I took a big sip of coffee. It was too hot. I swallowed it quickly to avoid burning my tongue and ended up burning my throat instead.

"Hiyah Markus! WOW! You look awful!" She put her hands on her hips. "Drinking too much? Did Darren keep you out late? I bet this is his fault." She was shaking her finger at me. How very motherly.

"No, it's not *his* fault. I bugged him to go for a beer." I blew in my coffee before I took another sip. "Besides, I'm old enough to know my limit."

Obviously, I wasn't.

Claire came around and rested her arm on my back as I leaned my head on the counter. "Oh, you poor thing." She said. "I wish I had some of my herbs here, I could brew you up something to make the hang-over go away." She rubbed my back a little. "But, I don't. I bet you could just *will* it away."

Her stress on the word 'will' seemed a little *too* significant. Neither Darren or I had included Claire in on what had happened, or what Darren was helping me practise. It was odd, almost like she knew my little *secret*.

I sighed. "I wish I could. But I don't have a connection to the other world like you do." Lifting my head up I turned to her. "Unless you want to give me your fairy friend's phone number. I could call him up and ask him to help me out."

"Well, I'm not supposed to give it out." She was clearly playing along now. "He might get terribly upset. He call-screens you know. But there is always texting." She grinned.

"Oh, does he? Well, I could always just send him a message."

"I don't know if he would call you back. He can be funny like that." Claire smiled and twisted a piece of hair in her fingers. The butterflies still in her hair, but pink ones today "Ooh, I forgot to show you Markus." She ran to the back of the store, making loud clip-clop noises. "I just got this. I am so EXCITED." She squealed. She returned and thrust a small pocket-size book towards me. It must have been used as it looked yellowed and abused.

I could barely read the faded cover. "Gram ...? Grimoire? What is it?"

"It's a spell book! I bought it yesterday in Salem. It was in an old shop, they were selling belongings from some dead person's house. Kinda sad, but it was my lucky day. Well, not for the dead person. But for me it was." Claire bubbled about her find.

"So, what are you going to do with it?" I flipped through the tattered pages, little notes hand written here and there on the pages. "Isn't this someone's diary?"

"No silly. It's a *spell* book." She held the little book to her chest like it was a kitten she just got for Christmas.

I believed in some magic-like things, my secret gift, but a spell book? What was next, would she take me out for a ride on her broom stick? "Okay. But what are you going to do with these so-called spells?"

"Well, uhmm, I will like, try them out of course."

"Couldn't that be dangerous Claire? Do you know what any of the spells are for?"

She looked down at her little book. "Of course I do. I read it all, a couple hundred times. Most of them are for protection, some for helping to find lost possessions, one of them for luck, another for money. But you should never ask for love or money, cause that bites you in the butt times three."

She seemed to know what she was talking about. I had read in one of my vampire books about the law of three fold: what you put out, comes back three times more. Not really something I would want to play around with.

"So, what spell are you going to try then?" I asked.

She thought for a moment. "I think there is one here about summoning an object. That sounds like an easy enough one to try. I don't think there's any danger there if I want to find or bring something of my own. I have nothing to gain from it, so there would be no harm in trying!"

"What of yours do you need?" I sipped my coffee.

"My light blue butterflies. I couldn't find them this morning, and since It is going to snow I always like to wear them for luck."

I shook my head and smiled at her. I had never come across anyone as strange as Claire.

"So, what do you have to do?"

"Uhm, just a sec ...Oh here." She found the page that she was looking for in her book. "It says we need something for the object to go into, like a box. Do we have that? Oh shoot, I should have been more prepared."

"Okay, hold on a minute." I turned around and looked under the counter, there was bound to be a box we could use. Sure enough, pushed to the back, was an old shoebox. "Here." I handed it to her. "Will this work?"

"I think so, I guess it would. I don't see why not. We can give it a try. Nothing to loose you know!" She dumped the contents of the box on the counter, old receipts held together in elastic bands. "Okay, next, we need ..." She read the page. "Okay, it says we should have a candle, that's not problem, we have plenty of those here. Just grab one of the tea lights behind you, Markus." I handed it to her. "Next, we need to identify the object we are looking for. Well, that is easy, we already did that. And then we just need to say the words. I'm so excited." She clapped her hands. "I bet this works. Just wait and see." She jumped up and down hugging her book.

I tried very hard to keep from laughing hysterically. I completely forgot about my headache or the hang over. This was going to be fun.

Suddenly, I felt bad for Claire. Some little book wouldn't make her lost butterfly hair clips appear in that box. I hope she didn't have her hopes set too high. I looked over to her. She was still smiling widely and now shaking the empty shoe box in anticipation. This was going to be awful, watching her get upset over something so silly. But she truly believed it, and it was making her so happy.

"Okay." I said "Let's give it a shot. What should I do?"

"Well, we put the box here." She sat it on a stool. "Then we each stand on opposite sides. And hold hands and chant. It shouldn't be that hard. The words are pretty easy."

As Claire put the lid on the box, I leaned over it just to make sure it was empty. We stood holding hands over top of it. She glanced at the page of her open book, and closed her eyes. "Okay Markus, repeat after me, but make sure you think of my butterfly clips.

Got it?" She opened her eyes and stared at me, her face serious. "Here we go ...uhhmm." She cleared her throat.

> "Bring me what I want.
> Bring me what I need.
> The object I ask for.
> Bring it to me.
> I ask of thee, I pray of thee.
> In this box fill it.
> I say so and will it."

We repeated the chant three times. I tried to concentrate on the clips, but all I could think of was "this had better damn well work." It had to, I didn't want to see the disappointment on Claire's face.

We let our hands drop away. My stomach felt sick, whether it was from last night's binge or nerves, I wasn't sure. Claire squeezed her eyes shut tight. "EEEEK! I just know this worked Markus." She reached down and lifted the lid off, her hands shaking.

We both peered down slowly.

Two light blue butterflies glittered in the box.

My jaw dropped. "Holly shit! It *did* work. But how?"

"See Markus. Magic *does* exist. You just have to believe, you know, you have to *want* it to happen. You need to *will* it." She picked up the two clips and placed them on her head. It looked like a butterfly breeding ground now. I watched her a moment longer as she patted them. She then started skipping and disappeared down one of the aisles.

I was shocked to say the least. I was getting used to the fact that I could use my gift and *will* – or I should say, predict – a chain of events. But this was different. Was it my will that made the clips appear? Or was it Claire's little spell? Maybe both? Who knows. I didn't know what to think. This was too bizarre.

Would Darren have an answer? On second thought, maybe it was better if I didn't tell him. He might kill me if he found out I was using my so-called gift for other purposes.

It would be best to keep *this* secret between Claire and I. At least for now.

Claire came back to the counter. "Wasn't that fun? We should try it again! What have you lost? What do you want to find Markus? Anything? Some vampire book maybe?"

The thought of peering into the little box and finding a long lost vampire book crossed my mind. It would be kind of cool and it could definitely be beneficial. But Darren's angry face crossed my mind again – just the thought of him finding out I used magic, my gift, or the combination of both relating to vampires in any way. I didn't think it would be a good idea. Plus, vampires were something that I obsessed over. What would happen if we were to do the spell again and my mind started concentrating on a real vampire showing up? Watching one slowly crawling out of the box, as much as I would love to see that, I knew it would be very bad.

Just thinking about it, I could feel my willing sensation stirring in my body. I stopped quickly.

"You know what Claire? I think I'll pass. This is all a little strange. Those aren't your spells anyway. What if they're bad?"

Claire nodded. "Okay. Well, your loss. These spells are fine. I don't think there is anything bad about them at all, or the fairies would have told me so. I just love magic! It's so much fun. And you didn't believe me."

"Oh brother." I shook my head.

Claire gave up. It was time for her to go home anyway. She did make a point of telling me that I *would* be assisting her with more magic, because she hadn't found anyone else it had worked for before. So I was stuck helping her out. "Great, lucky me." It was all I could get out. She left with her usual two handed wave good bye.

The store was completely empty except for me. The cold weather seemed to be keeping people away. I slid the empty shoe box back and forth between my hands. Did the magic *really* happen because of me? It was unsettling to think about. I didn't really believe in spells.

I tapped my fingers on the box. Do I try Claire's little spell? Would it hurt to? No, I shouldn't. I sat back down. In my indecision and frustration at wanting and not wanting to try magic again, I stared out the window.

It was dark out. I must have been in thought for a long while. The street lights were already on. There was a light snow starting to fall. It looked very peaceful. I enjoyed the snow. It made me happy.

My mind started to wonder thinking of winter days past, and ones yet to be. I knew Claire liked the snow. Did Darren? Would the slush on his expensive shoes bug him? Would the freezing cold

57

make him sick? He was always freezing cold anyway. I'm sure he detested the winter. I could picture him in a huge winter parka – or better yet, wrapped up like an Eskimo. The vision of it made me start to laugh.

"That would be a real sight to see."

Still amused with my thoughts, I got up off the stool and finally started to do some work around the store. There was some stock to put away, sweeping to be done, magazines to straighten up. The list went on. But it was my job after all.

The time passed quickly, and before I knew it, it was time to close up shop and head home. Getting my things from behind the counter, I noticed the shoe box still sitting, beckoning me. I rocked back and forth on my feet. "What the Hell." I said. "Might as well give it a try!"

I raised my hands over the box, setting firmly in mind my house keys. They would be the object I would summon. They were safe to think of. I started the words. "Bring to me the thing I have lost. Bring to me the thing to ..." The bell on the front door jingled. My concentration broke. In walked Darren, bag in one hand and coffee cup in another.

My arms drop quickly. "Hey Darren, what's up?" I must have looked like a deer in headlights, being caught doing something I shouldn't have.

"I thought I would be Mr. Nice Guy and bring you a coffee, a real coffee, not one of those awful ones you drink here all day." He nodded towards the coffee machine that sat behind me. "Markus, what were you doing with that box? You looked like you were in deep conversation with it. Have you given up communicating with fruit? Are you now onto cardboard products?" He smirked sitting the coffee and his bag on the counter.

"Well, the fruit just wasn't responding well lately." I smiled. "Thanks for the coffee." I sipped. It *was* really good. "I'm just locking up. Are you headed home or ...?"

"I had a few errands to run. But I'm finished now, so I am all yours. If you want me?" He paused. "Oh, how is your hang over? I had to drag you home from the pub. It's really amazing how much you weight."

"I still have a bit of a headache, but not too bad. Thanks for helping me home. I can't even remember getting there."

Darren leaned against the counter, grinning. "I'm not surprised, I thought you were part fish with the amount you had drank. You cost me a small fortune Mr. Cowboy."

I raised my eyebrow. "Mr. Cowboy? What is that supposed to mean?"

Darren's grin turned wicked. "I can honestly say I love seeing you intoxicated. You put on an accent and pretended to be a cowboy most of the way home. It was truly a sight to see."

"Oh god." My face blanched and my stomach turned. Darren's face became serious.

I raised my hand up. "I'm okay. Just embarrassed. Oh man. I really shouldn't drink so much. Next time will you please stop me?"

He snickered. "And ruin all my fun? If I am having to pay for the drinks, I might as well be entertained." Darren smirked. "Oh, by the way, I had seen this today and thought you might like it." He handed me the small bag he was carrying. I put my hand in and pulled out bright red fabric. It was a scarf, simple, and soft. I was sure that since Darren had purchased it, it must have been expensive. It was nice, I liked it. I was sure to stand out among all the black and grey heavy coats in the winter weather.

"Thanks Darren. This is awesome." I hung it around my neck. "I've never worn a scarf before – I just pull up my hood."

He came over to me and adjusted the scarf, looping and tying it. "Well now, that's better. I'm glad you like it. It will make it easier for me to *look out* for you. A grey wool coat would look sharp on you too. I suppose there is always Christmas." He was obviously pleased that I liked his gift.

"Christmas." I mumbled. "Yah, I suppose that is coming up. What are you doing? Going home to visit your family?" I put my coat on and grabbed my knapsack off the floor. Christmas was enjoyable, the music, the decorations and the snow. But in my foster care, it was never much of anything. Too many Christmas mornings were spend with no gifts.

Darren picked up on my sadness. "I should visit my family, but I have not decided as of yet. What are your plans, Markus?"

"Uhmm, I think I'm going to work. I could use the cash. Besides, I don't have any family, so it will give me a chance to get caught up on some things, you know." It must have sounded pathetic, but it was the true.

We left the store. I took a deep breathe of the cold snowy air. "It's so fresh; I like the winter. Hey, this scarf is actually keeping my neck warm. Good thinking, Darren."

"Anytime. I also enjoy winter. It's my most favourite of the seasons. Everything covered in a blanket of white, holiday cheer, festivities at every corner, people dressed in coloured layers. The smells drift through the air. Truly wonderful." He stared into the distance as we walked.

"Aren't you just poetic Darren." I punched him lightly in the shoulder. "So, you hungry? I am starved. Ooh, fish and chips, I could totally go for that." I patted my stomach.

"I've already had my meal. But I'll keep you company as you ingest grease. There is a chip shop I know of. It looks like a little dive, but it's apparently the best fish and chips around. It's a bit of a walk to get there, but it is a nice night after all, and I do love walking in the snow. Also I have a request, no beer tonight for you. I can't stand the thought of you vomiting again." He wrinkled his nose.

"Ha. Ha. Ha. Very funny." I responded, then continued. "So, what did you eat for dinner?"

"I had my liquids again. Fresh hot soup. Was not the best stock, but it hit the spot."

Darren seemed to enjoy his soup. I think that must be all he ever ate.

"You know, you might want to consider eating solids once in a while, maybe you won't be as cold! Besides, it helps put hair on your chest. You know, maybe you'll be more of a man."

Everything flashed.

I didn't see it coming.

Darren had my face in a pile of snow before I could blink. I didn't think anyone could move that fast. He lifted me up with ease and turned me over. "More of a man, huh?" He was starting to laugh loudly. "I'll show you more of a man." Darren picked me up and threw me in the snow bank again. Clearly, he was enjoying this.

Judging by his sheer strength, he was definitely more of a man than he appeared.

"Alright! Alright! You are more man than I will ever be." I was laughing and wiping the snow from my face. It was cold but it melted from the heat of my skin. I held my arm up towards Darren for help. "Geesh, you wait. I'll get you back for that when you least expect it, Darren."

"Oh, really? I would like to see that." He was in a lighter mood as he wiped the snow from the back of my coat. "Okay, let's go get you some food, I think you need to eat some solids so you can try to be more of a challenge to me."

"Okay. But you know, you only won, because I wasn't prepared. The scarf you got me blew into my face and blocked my view."

"Keep telling yourself that Markus." He chuckled. "Oh, how is Claire doing? I spotted her earlier this evening. She was happily skipping through the snow. She definitely is an odd girl. I know she doesn't care for me."

"She likes you. She just doesn't know you well like I do."

It was true. Claire didn't usually have anything nice to say about Darren. She usually blamed him for anything wrong in my life. It bothered me that he was the only thing she was ever negative about. Not that her dislike made a difference to me. But it would have been good to have my only two friends like each other.

I turned to answer his question. "She bought some book, a grim-oh-er, something like that. She was trying it out."

"A Grimoire? Markus? Is that what it was?"

"Yah, she went to some old house in Salem where they were selling off some dead guy's stuff. She bought it there and it had all of these spells. We tried one out. It was harmless. It worked though, so cool. We made her lost hair clips reappear. I couldn't believe it myself, but it really did work." Getting excited I got caught up in my story. I shouldn't have let it slip.

Darren clenched his jaw. His face wore a mixture of anger, shock and horror. "Markus. Are you crazy? What did I tell you? Don't you listen to anything I say?"

"I did. I was careful. There was a spell to say and we had to specifically ask for and think of the hair clips for it to work. Nothing went wrong. Don't worry about it."

"Don't worry? You know how dangerous that stuff is? Do you? Mixed with what you can do, I don't even want to think what would happen!"

We were stopped on some dark, narrow side street.

"Darren, just relax okay. Nothing happened. Okay? It was fun stuff only. I'm not going to do something stupid like you automatically assume I will. I'm not dumb you know." My arms folded, I felt a little defensive.

"Well, considering you do things like this, that doesn't sound like something an intelligent person would do."

"Fuck you, Darren!" Anger coursed through me. He seemed to always be the one telling me what to do. It was my gift, and if I wanted to try a few spells with it, so what? What did he know about it? How did he become the expert?

I let out other thoughts before I could filter what I was saying:" You're just mad because you can't do things like I can. Maybe you're jealous! Is that why you don't like Claire? She can do some magic and you can do nothing? Your money can get you everything, but can't buy you that?" My fists clenched, I ground my teeth.

Darren stood in the shadows, silent. So mad, he was contemplating beating me to death. It wouldn't be the first time someone tried.

"Markus." His teeth were clenched. "I only warn you to keep you from getting hurt or from someone else getting hurt. Don't you understand that? There are things out there that you cannot possibly imagine. Things that I don't want you to ever see." His head dropped.

My temper still flared. "What? So you want to keep me from seeing what you rich people have, huh? How's that fair? So what? You're afraid I will get famous or something from my gift as you call it and then I get to live in your world? Is that it? What, people with money don't care about anyone and are cold? Cold like you ? It that what you want to keep me from?"

"Markus, you are wrong." His voice was slow and methodical. "That's not what I meant. I just want you to watch what you are doing. Bad things can happen, there can be dangers. Don't you realize that?"

"You know Darren, it's not about what you want. I can do anything I want you know."

I was starting to shout. "If I want to try something then I will! If I want a blood thirsty vampire to come here and chase me down so I can have an immortal life, then I will make it happen. It's not up to you. I will do as I please. It is *my* will. I have nobody to worry about. No one cares about me, so what does it matter?"

My body was shaking now. I felt a pulling and pulsing inside, tears welled in my eyes. It was the first time it ever dawned on me how awful it felt to never have had someone love me, or worry about me. I had felt alone all my life.

"Markus, that is not true." Darren moved towards me slowly. "I care about you, I ...I mean, you are my best friend. So don't think that way." He tried to put his arm around my shoulders, but I stepped away.

"Leave me alone, Darren." I was crying. I didn't want to be. I wanted to go home. "Just leave me alone."

I ran. Down the side street and around the corner. Eventually my run slowed to a fast walk. I was still angry with Darren, but at the same time angry with myself. He was my best friend, he always helped me out. This was how I repaid him? No wonder I was alone and always would be.

CHAPTER FOUR

PUSH

I kept my head down to keep the snow from hitting my eyes as it came down thicker. It was turning into the city's first blizzard. Faster, I walked as though my pace would keep the cold away from me. There was only the odd person here and there on the strange snow-covered streets as I wandered aimlessly; I wasn't really paying attention; I didn't care. I needed to clear my head. Looking down at my feet I kicked at the snow as I continued. Guilt consumed me after lashing out at Darren. I was so stupid.

The wind blew harder, a cold gust caught my scarf and sent it flying off my neck. From the wrestling in the snow or during my tantrum it had loosened. I turned to run after it. The wind wouldn't give it up, and it flitted and floated down the street.

I ran for a number of blocks. Finally, the scarf caught itself on a piece of metal protruding from the side of a building. I changed my pace to a walk, out of breath from my sprint.

Bending over, I reached down and lifted the scarf, giving it a quick shake before putting it back around my neck. I wasn't sure how Darren had tied it. It had looked easy enough, but all I could mange was a thick knot. It would do. I didn't want to loose it again.

I looked around. It was clear I had no idea where I was. This place was strange and I didn't recognise it. There wasn't a single soul around. It was still and quiet with only the snow making any movement. The buildings were old and in need of major repair. All abandoned because there were no lights in any of the shattered windows or broken down doors. My body trembled.

Turning around I started walking back the way I came. I crossed the open square that once had been a parking lot. There were two streets that opened up at the end. I wasn't sure which one I had come in from. My foot prints should have been in the piling snow, but the wind was so fierce it swept them away.

I walked towards the one on the right. It looked to be more sheltered from the snowy blizzard. If I got lost, I knew I would eventually find a street I was familiar with, or a train station, or a taxi as a last resort, although I didn't have much cash on me. I tightened my scarf and jacket.

It was bloody freezing. My teeth chattered. I began to walk. I wanted to be at home.

Half way down the narrow back street I heard a odd noise. Foot steps? That wasn't it. Maybe more of a scraping sound? Not sure, I looked around. No one but me. I started to walk faster and turned right at the next street. I had no idea if I was going in a good direction, but I just wanted to get into public view again. Everything was too quiet and scary.

The empty street narrowed and arched to right. I followed it. The scraping sound still continued. Whatever it was, I hoped to hell it would stop, because I was scared shitless!

The street abruptly ended after the bend. There was no other way to continue. It was a dead end that stopped at the entrance to an old building. I thought briefly about going inside and slipping out the back door to a parking lot, or hoped it might exit onto another street with some people on it. But going through a dark old building alone at night in the middle of nowhere didn't appeal to me.

I turned, and the scraping sound came sharply close. I jumped. I couldn't see anyone, not even an animal. It must of been the wind, blowing a piece of metal maybe? My body shivered. I started to walk back up the street from where I came.

That is when I saw him.

Leaning against the wall of one of the deserted buildings, a man wearing sunglass and what looked like jeans, a white hooded sweater, and white matching baseball cap. He had a long piece of metal piping in his hand which he scraped back and forth on the ground. I now knew where the sound was coming from, but it didn't make me feel any better. He kept his head down looking at his feet.

My first impulse was to hurry past him – he was obviously up to no good – and when he was out of sight I would make a run for it. Tension filled me. I started to walk, trying to stay close to the opposite side of the narrow street. My heart was beating fast. The wind blew a cold gust of snow into my face. For a moment, I was blinded. Something hit the front of my body, as though I hit the wall. I bounced off the cement and fell to the ground.

I open my eyes and heard a voice. "So sorry buddy, but you should really watch where you're going. Maybe don't walk so fast. What's your hurry anyway?" The man was squatting by my feet.

Shivering, I managed to respond. "Sorry, I got snow in my eyes and couldn't see. Sorry."

"Don't be sorry buddy. Too much submission takes all the fun out of it. You don't want to spoil my fun do you?"

"No, sorry ...I mean no, I don't." My heart raced, I was shaking now. What did he mean by 'fun'?

He stood up and walked towards my head. He bent down and grabbed me by my knotted scarf. With one hand he pulled my body up off the ground and set me back on my feet. I went rigid with fear.

"There you go buddy, back on your feet. No worries. I won't hurt you. I won't bite. *Yet.*"

He snickered, a deep mean sound, it was pure evil. Why did I run away from Darren? I wish he were here to help me now. My hands were shaking, nausea swept over me and my lip quivered. Tears welled in my eyes. I only had one though: I was going to die.

"What do you want from me?" I almost begged. "I only have a few bucks on me but you can have them. Just leave me alone. Please!"

"Ahh, buddy, what would I want with your money? I have no use for it. But, I'd like you to make this fun for me. It's no fun when you stand here shaking in your boots buddy. So do me a favour. RUN!"

The stranger pushed me from behind. I slid a few feet forward and then ran. I pushed my body as hard as I could and raced for my life. Everything was blurry but I didn't care. I just needed to get away from him.

Everything swirled.

I fell backwards to the ground. It was like I ran head first into the wall again. This time my eyes were open, so I could see that it wasn't a wall. It was the strange man. He felt lie a wall; his body was hard and cold as concrete. As fast as I had fallen, I was yanked to my feet. "Buddy, you can do better than that. Come on, give it a better try." He said pushing me forward again.

I ran. Fear fuelled me.

It took all my strength to run. I was short of breath, my heart racing. I had to keep going. I needed to get away from this guy. A cross street was coming up, if I could just make it a little further. Hopefully, there were people around. My limbs ached and my muscles throbbed.

I reached the adjoining street. Empty. I kept going.

This time the stranger appeared out of thin air in front of me, and I couldn't stop myself, I crashed into his body. I fell backwards and slid across the ground. My body was weak. No strength to run again. This was the end, I had nothing left in me but to cry and give in.

Tears streamed down my face.

He laughed his evil laugh. "Oh buddy, is this it? Is that the best you could do? Well, I must say, I enjoyed myself a little." He pulled me off the ground by my jacket collar. This time he didn't stand me on my feet, but he actually held me in the air about a foot off the ground. I could see most of his face now, almost perfect and smooth, pale complexion and a wide smile. His eyes were hidden behind sunglasses that reflected my dread-filled face. He seemed strangely familiar. His white teeth glimmered. Perfect, white teeth.

"Buddy, you have any last words? Any confessions? Anything at all?" The cold smile got bigger as he started to bring my face closer to his own.

A loud crash echoed in my ears. I hit the wall again. This time it was both the stranger and I. We crashed to the ground. He lost his grip on me and I rolled away. Snow blew and stung my eyes. I wiped them, I needed to see so I could run.

I was surprised to see the stranger being lifted off the ground. He was thrown head first into the wall across the street. He fell with a thud. As fast as he had fallen, he was already back on his feet. Chills crept down my back. The stranger was about to run at his assailant, but didn't. He was on one side of the street and the next second he was locking arms with another man. They were evenly matched. I knew the strength of the stranger. I thought it was impossible for anyone to match that, but apparently not.

The two men twisted and turned. Finally, the white hooded stranger threw the other man into the wall over my head where I sat frozen in the snow. I heard the crunch, and the brick crumbled. I knew the second man must be dead. The impact would have been too much for anyone to survive.

The man's body fell to the ground. But like my attacker, the stranger easily pulled himself up. He turned and looked at me. Darren's eyes stared into mine, a stare that penetrated my soul.

The white hooded stranger flew at Darren, lifted him up and slammed him into the wall again. My blood began to rush. Anger pulsed through me. There was no way in hell this monster would kill Darren. Darren was my friend. Darren came to save me. I wouldn't let this asshole kill him. My body tensed.

I stood up and faced my attacker. "GET THE FUCK AWAY FROM US." I bellowed. He stopped his assault on Darren and turned towards me.

"Ohh, buddy, what are you going to do? Yell at me? Maybe try to ask me to stop nicely? You can't hurt me!" He lurched towards me.

Darren looked up, his eyes now wide with terror at the realization of what was about to happen.

The stranger came at me fast. With an adrenaline rush I swung my arm up hitting into his side while trying to block him as he bared down on me. He stumbled against the wall. My anger still coarsed through my veins, as did the shock that I managed to throw him off. The stranger growled. "Lucky shot, buddy. But I've had enough of you!"

He lunged at me again. I was crushed to the ground, and the wind was knocked out of my lungs. Darren was lying over top of me. He had somehow thrown himself in front of the stranger and taken the brunt of the impact.

He pulled himself off me and stared into my face, concerned, that split second was all it took. The white hooded attacker grabbed Darren and heaved him. I forced myself off the ground and ran to him to shield him from the attacker.

The hooded stranger looked viciously at me and spat. "And now you *will* die!" He ran at me full force.

My anger pulsed and swelled in my body and I clenched my fist. A gust of icy snow pelted my eyes, forcing me to close them. When I tried to see again so I could defend myself, the stranger was gone.

I stood motionless for a moment. Then I looked to the ground where Darren had been. He wasn't there. He was already standing at my side. He reached over and caught me in a hard embrace. It forced the air out of my lungs. I never realized how strong he actually was.

He let go and smiled at me. "You alright, Markus? Let's get you home. You look frozen to the bone."

'Yah, I'm fine. Just a little ..." I shook.

He reached over and dusted the snow from my head, and then wiped it from my face. "Don't worry, Markus. Let's just get you warm."

We started to walk. Both of us silent. Considering what had happened, I wasn't scared anymore. I felt safe because Darren was here. My best friend had come to my rescue. I knew he would never let anyone, or anything, hurt me – I don't know why, but I knew it was true.

Someone in this world actually cared.

I was tired and hungry. But I was safe.

For now.

#

CHAPTER FIVE

We walked in silence, both of us in deep thought. I replayed the night's events in my mind. How did it all happen? The stranger was so fast, so strong. But then again, I was so cold and so tired and fearful. Maybe it all seemed more than it really had been? It was all strange. Who would want to hurt me? Did he really want to do that? Was he just trying to scare me?

Deep down I knew that the stranger had meant to kill me.

But how did Darren find me? I watched his body slam into the wall again in my mind. He should have been dead from that impact. A shiver ran through my body. I couldn't believe he had come to save me. Would I have been done for if he hadn't? I felt fear and pride as he fought my attacker.

My mind raced again. This time wondering what happened to the attacker? My eyes were closed when he disappeared, so I had no answer. I was tired now, in fact the cold had chilled my entire body. I started to shiver violently, my knees buckled. Everything in my view brighten and then went dark. I fell to the ground.

My dreams were grey and dark. Horses trotted in circles around me. Panicked, I tried to grab a hold of something. I needed to run. I needed to escape. I tried to grasp at the horses. They were too fast. Round and round they went. I was nauseous from spinning.

A hand reached down from nowhere and pulled me up onto one of the wild beasts. I felt warmth. I felt safe. I felt like I could get away. The horse I was on broke free from the others and we sped away ...

I awoke.

The room was lit with a soft warm light, heat radiated from the fire place. I was disoriented. I hadn't a clue where I was. Panic set in. An odd sensation – ice cold – ran through my hair. I tried to sit up, but the cold held me down. It felt like a hand holding me in place. Then I heard the voice. "Markus, it's okay. You're here with me. Don't be afraid."

I rolled my eyes around to see Darren sitting behind me. His hand slid off my chest where it held me in place, his other stopped stroking the top of my head. His face twisted, contorted. Anger, then resolve. Calmness returned along with his usual steady gaze.

I sat upright on the couch where I was laying. The room was dark with panelled walls and a ceiling lined with heavy timbers. Arched floor to ceiling French-doors were opposite the fireplace. Through the glass in the darkness, thick snow covered trees.

Fear washed over me. Where am I? What happened to me? Darren stood up from the couch where he was sitting and loomed over me. "Markus, please don't be alarmed. You are suffering from shock. You're safe. You're at my home, and I will not let anything happen to you." Anxiety spread across his face. He could tell I noticed his indecision and his face relaxed, as though playing a role. "Markus, you need to eat. I'll be back in a moment with something for you." He turned and left the room.

He was right. I felt the pain of hunger in my stomach. My head throbbed. I wasn't sure what was real and what wasn't. How did I get here? What time is it? Why am I at Darren's home? My mind raced. The memory of the fight came rushing back. I stood up quickly, my legs a little weak, my stomach turned. I walked towards the windows. I felt like I was going to be sick. I pressed my forehead against the glass, the cool was soothing, but not as much as the cold comfort as Darren's hand.

I looked outside. It seemed Darren's house was in the middle of nowhere. We were surrounded by miles of trees, nothing else, no lights in the distance. The panic started again. Where was Darren? What if my attacker found us? What if he was trying to kill Darren right now? I turned and walked quickly to the door of the room.

Before I could get there, the knob turned and it opened. Darren stood in the opening holding a tray. He smiled. My body relaxed. I walked back to the couch and plunked down. Exhausted, I rested my head in my hands.

Darren moved my arms and put the tray on my lap, then sat beside me. "You alright Markus? You really had me worried there. You have been out for hours." He folded his hands together and patiently waited for my response.

"Oh, yah, I'm fine." It was all I managed to say. I looked down at the steaming thick soup on the tray. Hunger took over me and I ate.

Darren sat as I downed my meal like a starved prisoner finally rescued. I didn't even take a breath between spoonfuls. Finally, I set the tray down on the coffee table.

"Thanks." I smiled at him and leaned back against the comfy couch. "Nice place you've got, Darren. Do your parents know I'm here?"

He smiled. "You're welcome. I'm glad you like my home. But, no, my parents are in Europe, so they don't know that you're here."

He seemed to relax a little.

"Darren." I said. "Can I ask you something?"

He raised his eyebrow. "Yes, what would you like to know?"

"Well, uhmm ..." I paused. "What happened? I remember we

were walking, then I woke up here. Did I black out or something? And how did we get here?"

He took a breath. "After the attack, we started to walk, I wanted to get you some place safe, but, you must have been so hungry and exhausted that you passed out. I'm sure that it was from shock as well. So I carried you to my car and drove here. I was a little worried that your attacker would know where you lived, so I thought it would be safer for you to be here with me."

"How would that crazy guy know where I lived?" I was a little confused.

"Markus, I am positive that he would know where you live. I'm sure he would have tracked you down. As a matter of fact, I am certain that he has already been there."

I shifted a bit on the couch. "How? I mean, I never told him my address." I felt my back pocket. "I still have my wallet, so how could that creep know where I live?"

Darren's face appeared worried. "Markus, What do you remember of the fight?"

"Well, I was lost, then the guy hit me, then he helped me up and made me run. He kept chasing me down, then you came and surprised him and you two started to scrap it out. Then he came at me again, or at least I think he did, and he took off."

"I see." Darren nodded. "But do you remember anything that seemed strange about it at all?"

I frowned and shook my head."No, I don't."

"For the best anyhow. This has been a big shock to you. I think you should try to sleep again. You still don't seem to be 100 percent yet."

Darren got up from the couch. He walked to a chair that sat beside the fire and grabbed a thick quilted blanket and brought it to me. He then picked up the tray from the table and walked to the door. Pausing briefly, he turned to me and smiled weakly. His eyes gave him away: he was concerned.

I stared after him as he closed the door. Loneliness set in again, tainted with fear. I knew he was only a room or so away, but I would have preferred him to stay with me. I could have asked him to, but, I couldn't bring myself to do it.

I shook the blanket open and spread it over myself. I wasn't cold at all. The fire was very warm, but I needed that feel of security around me. I wasn't tired, so I gazed into the flames. My eyes became very heavy, the exhaustion came again. It didn't feel natural. It felt medicated, but I was too sleepy to give it any other thought. I closed my eyes and slept.

It was light outside when I woke up. The skies were grey and snow swirled around. It was serene, but forsaken. My eyes took in the view and then I turned to face the fire. It was still burning warm and bright. Cheerful and comforting. It was what I needed. Now that it was light out, I could see more of the room. The walls had dark wood paneling. Bookcases lined the wall of the fireplace. There must have been thousands of books. I got up and took a closer look. Titles and languages that seemed unfamiliar to me. There was the occasional novel that I did recognize, but not many. Some of the books must have been hundreds of years old. I fought off the temptation to pull one off the shelf. I knew they must have been worth a lot of money, so I left them alone. The rest of the room was simple.

My stomach started to growl, I put my hands over it attempting to quiet it. It didn't work. I decided to go in search of Darren. He might not have wanted to disturb me. But I was awake and hungry now, so it would be fine. I was also curious to see more of his house. I was sure it would be large and grand.

I walked slowly out to the hall. It was tall and wide and lined with the same wood panelling. I came to a staircase going downwards. There were two, one on each side of the large front hall. Down below sat a round table in the middle of the grand entrance, and at the furthest end, two heavy wooden doors which I guessed to be the front doors. A monstrous chandelier hung overhead. This place must have cost a fortune.

Looking away from the main entrance, I continued on my path down the hallway. There was a door to the left. I stopped and knocked softly before opening it. It was a bathroom. I continued to the end of the hall where there was one last door. It must be a bedroom. There were only three doors on this floor. Hopefully it was Darren's room.

Again, I knocked gently. The door swung open because it wasn't closed all the way. I poked my head in – there were large windows on the opposite wall, a couch sat in front of them. In the middle of the room, a bed. Clothes strewn across it, like someone was sorting through them.

Two doors were on the other interior wall, maybe closets? I didn't bother to check. The iron circular staircase that lead to another floor above caught my attention. I climbed them and wound my way, realizing how high the ceilings were. At the top was an entire glass room, except for one wall and the beamed ceiling. Two couches and a chair sat in the middle of this aquarium-like room, perfect for taking in the view. It was high above the forest, like it was built on stilts. I walked to the window and gazed out. Shades of green as far as I could see. It was a sea of trees, frosted with glistening icy snow. Sunlight reflected off it all, creating bright sparkles. I gasped at the beauty.

I heard soft breathing. "Do you like it, Markus?" Darren said from behind me. "This was a widows peak. The wives of sailors would watch for the return of their husbands' ships from here."

He rose from the arm chair where he sat. I don't know why I didn't see him at first. I was sure the room was empty. He wore track pants and nothing else. He walked over and planted himself directly in front of me, which seemed merely inches away. My heart raced and pounded hard. My eyes wandered down at his chest, his rippling stomach. His tanned yet pale complexion, he was perfect.

"Do you like the view Markus?" He purred. His face had a mischievous grin. "Do you?"

The blood rushed to my face. "Uhmm, yes, I do. It's uhmm, really beautiful." Embarrassed and unsure of what to do I stood still. He was so close to me – icy coolness radiated from him – I couldn't catch my breathe.

He stepped away and turned to look out the window. I was relieved. I could breath, but I also didn't want him to be far from me. I surveyed him, his muscular back facing me now. So smooth, defined, almost inhumanly sublime.

I gave my head a shake. "Your home is really nice, Darren. I didn't mean to snoop around, but I was kinda hungry and was looking for you."

He turned back towards me. "Of course you're hungry. I'll get you something to eat. As for peeking around, please feel free. I haven't had someone in my home in a very long time. It's nice to have the company." He looked out the window again and sighed.

"Well, I'm not sure I could go back to my apartment now, not after seeing how amazing your house is! You must think I live in a hole."

"No, I do not think that, Markus. I'm grateful for your company. I feel life in your apartment. My home is cold and hollow. You're welcome to stay here for awhile. But unfortunately nothing permanent." His jaw clenched at his own last statement, anger flashed in his eyes.

I didn't know what he was thinking. Nor would I have the chance to ask as my stomach interrupted with a loud rumbling. "Oh, boy. Sorry. I guess I am hungrier than I thought."

He smiled. "Okay, let's go to the kitchen to get you something to eat."

Darren headed towards the metal stairs, and I followed. "So Darren, is this your room? It's awesome."

"Yes, it is."

I assumed he wasn't blown away by how amazing it really was.

We walked past the clothing scattered bed. "I guess it's laundry day? Or are you really a slob when it comes to clothes, hmm? Gotta have one bad habit don't you?" I teased.

He walked in front of me, his bare back fully exposed, still catching my attention. "No, I am not a slob, Markus. I'm sorting as I will be taking a holiday to visit family for the winter break. I'll be leaving shortly."

I felt hurt. He hadn't told me about that. He mentioned there was a possibility, but he never confirmed. True, I wasn't his keeper, so he had every right to spend the holiday with his loved ones. I was jealous – not so much because he had a family and I didn't, but that his family was able to spend time with him.

Why was I frustrated now? He was my friend and it was his life. I had to stop thinking this way. I knew it was because he saved my life, so I naturally wanted him around to keep me safe. I put my thoughts away. "So, where are you going then?"

We walked down the stairs to the main entrance and through a set of doors that led into a large kitchen. It had an all-glass back wall, three stone walls and large appliances and a fireplace. My jaw dropped at the very sight of it.

"Well, my family is in London at the moment, so I will be going there." He went to the fridge and pulled out a carton of eggs and some cheese.

"Oh, that sounds like a pretty cool trip. When do you leave?" I feigned a smile.

He was mixing ingredients now. "Today. Did you want coffee?"

He was leaving today? Darren put down the mixing bowl and went to the counter to pour the coffee. He stirred it and brought it over to me. I took it gratefully. "I could get used to this service."

He grinned.

"Here." He pulled out a high stool that tucked into the kitchen island where he was about to cook. "Please sit." He padded the seat.

"Thanks. Keep this up Dare and you'll never get rid of me."

"Dare?" His eyebrow raised in curiousity. "What's with that?"

"Oh, sorry, just a habit. I like to abbreviate names."

He continued to work at the eggs, which looked to be the beginning of an omelette.

I shifted in my seat. "Uhmm, on your way to the airport, would it be possible for you to drop me off at my place?"

Darren stopped what he was doing and stared at me. "Why? I told you it's not safe there."

"I know that. But I need to sleep somewhere, and it's my home after all." The nightmare of my attack flashed in my mind. I got sidetracked this morning so I could push the horrible memories away. I refocused. "Dare I need my clothes, and I do have to go to work you know."

The slight flexing of his chest and stomach caught my attention. "Markus, I called your work, and let them know you won't be coming in as you are taking a holiday. Also, I have clothes for you." He went back to his cooking.

I sat, confused. "What? I don't get it. I'm not going on holiday ... or, am I staying here while you're gone?"

Darren looked at me, his eyes had that sparkle once again. "No, you will not be staying here while I am gone. You're coming with me to London. I'm not letting you out of my sight, not even for a moment."

I wasn't expecting that. "Really? You're joking right? I can't afford to go there!"

He grinned. "It's my treat Markus. Besides, it would do you well to experience a little of the world. As long as you don't mind me being there with you?"

"Mind? Why the hell would I mind? This is going to be so cool!"

I was thrilled, Darren looked very please. "Well, let's get some food in you, and then we can start packing. Okay? And by the way, I already have your passport. I grabbed it from your apartment a week ago. I was planning to surprise you with this trip."

"That's awesome, Dare!" I must have been oozing excitement. "So, do you have it all planned out what we are doing, exploring all sorts of things like that? Oh, but you are there to visit your family too, so I guess if you give me a map or something, I can wander around."

"Are you crazy?" He choked. "I will *not* let you wonder the streets of a strange country all on your own. You are my guest, you can visit and meet my family. That will only be brief anyhow, so basically the whole time I'm yours."

An omelette appeared in front of me, and Darren at my side. I didn't even notice him walk from the other side of the island to where I sat.

His bare, chilled, washboard stomach rubbed against my arm as he reached across the island, grabbing the salt and pepper. He placed them by my plate. He leaned in and whispered in my ear. "Eat." Darren retracted and walked towards the glass windows at the back of the kitchen.

I blushed as fiery thoughts ran through my head, but I picked up my fork and began to eat.

Famished I finished in surprising speed, maybe due to hunger or maybe the excitement at the thought of my first real trip.

I pushed the plate away and stood up. Darren picked it up and put it in the dishwasher. "Time for you to go and get yourself cleaned up, Markus. I believe you know where the shower is?"

"Yup." I nodded. "I do. I guess I need a towel."

"I'll bring you one. I'm going to clean the kitchen up a bit first, so go ahead and I'll bring it up. And also, you will find everything you need, shampoo and such are there for your use."

Darren continued his cleaning as I walked out of the kitchen. He scrubbed the counter forcefully, as though he was angry for some reason. Maybe I insulted him? I didn't know.

Up to the bathroom I went. In the shower I let the hot water bead off of me. It felt good, relaxing. Finally, I finished and shut off the water. There on the counter sat a towel, toiletries and a change of clothes.

After dressing, I packed up my things and made my way to Darren's room. The door was open. I walked in. Darren, now fully clothed, sat on the couch, two suitcases at his side. "Ready, Markus? I know it's early, but I like to stay ahead of schedule. Besides, I need a drink before we fly, takes the edge off."

"I'm in for that! Where should I put this stuff?" I held up the old clothes and the bag. He stood up and took both, then tossed the clothes on the floor and put the bag in one of the suitcases.

Darren grabbed the handles of both suitcases, picked them up and started towards the door of his room. "Okay." He said. "Let's go."

I walked over to him quickly to help with the luggage – either they were extremely light, or Darren was putting on a good show of making them look easy to carry. "Here, let me take one of those."

I reached for the handle, touching his cold hand. He relaxed his grip for only a moment at the shock of my hand against his. I briefly felt the true heaviness of the suitcase. There was no way in hell I could make carrying them look easy. Darren tightened his grip again and headed to the front door.

He stopped in the front hall. "Could you open the door please?"

"Sure." I walked past him and pulled at the handle. The door was solid as concrete, but I managed to swing it open. A cold gust of wind swept into the house, and I shivered a little. I hadn't realized how cozy and warm it was inside.

The front of the house had a huge overhang. It was large enough to cover a few vehicles. An SUV and car were parked there. Both were black with tinted windows and looked expensive. Darren walked towards the SUV. He opened up the back and effortlessly placed each bag into the vehicle. Then opened the driver's side door.

"Markus? Are you going to stand there or are you coming?" He got into the vehicle.

I followed suit and got in. "Uhmm, shouldn't you lock your front door?"

"No, it will automatically lock, don't worry about it. Besides, not very many neighbours around here."

With that he put on his sunglasses and began to drive. It wasn't that bright out, but I suppose they were fashionable.

The road leading away from his home was winding and well maintained. Only a little dusting of snow covered it. The shelter of the thick trees most likely helped.

We arrived at the airport a couple of hours later. Traffic seemed to have slowed us down. We made our way through the terminal to the lounge. Darren got me a drink and then excused himself to make a call in private. He was gone about 40 minutes. I didn't mind. I was preoccupied with a crossword puzzle I found in an abandoned newspaper.

When he came back, he brought with him some lunch for me, as well as aother beer. I was starting to enjoy this. We sat for awhile longer, then boarded the plane. Our seats were in first class. Nausea overtook me – I had never flown before, so my fear was starting to surface.

Darren sat beside me, looking calm. He handed me a tiny pill and a bottle of water. "It will help you relax. No worries, I won't let anything happen to you." He turned and faced the front of the plane.

I swallowed the pill, drank the water and closed my eyes. I couldn't believe how nervous I was. Was I the only one feeling this way? I tried to take deep breaths.

The engines started, everyone was seated. The stewardess voice echoed on the P.A. system. I couldn't make out what she was saying, my ears were ringing. We were starting to move. I felt warm, too warm, I was getting very uncomfortable, beads of sweat were forming over my face. There was pressure now, forcing us all back in our seats. "Oh god." It was all I could say.

There was a sudden coldness against the back of my neck. It soothed the uncomfortable heat. I opened my eyes, Darren was looking at me with a slightly amused expression, and his hand was outstretched holding the back of my neck. "Are you going to be okay, Markus? Try to breathe and relax, it'll be fine."

I let out a slow breath. "Okay. I'm fine." Closing my eyes again, I leaned back in my seat. Darren's ice cold hand remained – the coolness quenched the nauseous heat. We remained like that until I fell asleep.

CHAPTER SIX
ALEX

The flight was long, but not so bad. I had slept through a fair bit, because Darren's pill was apparently a sleep aid. It definitely did the trick.

After we landed, we were shuffled down numerous halls of the airport. I was confused and unsure where we were going, because I had never done this before. Darren made his way with ease.

Finally, we were ushered through a set of doors into a parking lot. There sat a car complete with a driver. "Is that for us?" Considering it was only Darren and I here, I could have answered my own question.

He wheeled his luggage over to the driver who took it without question. "Markus, come on." He motioned me over.

Once we were seated, the driver drove without instruction. I was excited to see the sights as we made our way, but the windows were so darkly tinted, I wasn't able to see much of anything at all. Disappointed, I leaned back into my seat.

We drove fast – people, buildings, flashed by. I didn't know what the time was, and besides, there was a six hour time change. It looked like it was evening, but it could have been early morning for all I knew. It was possible to ask Darren, but the entire drive he remained motionless, quiet, giving the impression he wanted to be left alone.

The cityscape disappeared and the fertile country spread out ahead of us. Gentle rolling hills, lush green, tall grasses as far as my eyes could see. I wanted to get out of the car to stretch and breath it all in. But there wasn't much chance of that happening I was sure. So I tried to stretch the best I could in my seat. My discomfort seemed to catch Darren's attention. "Are you alright Markus? We're almost there, so can you hold on for a little longer?"

"Yah, for sure. But being stuck in that plane, then the car ... I'm getting a little claustrophobic. Where are we going anyway?"

His eyes peered outside before answering. "It's a little estate getaway. It's very quiet and removed. You know how I like such places. We'll spend a few days there, have a brief visit with my family and then we'll have some time in the city for you to enjoy. Does that work for you?"

"That works! So, how much longer until we get there?" I smiled childlike.

"Another few minutes." He shook his head. "What am I going to do with you?"

"Well, for starters, I think you're gonna have to feed me. After that, I'll let you know."

I felt more comfortable now, but at the same time a little nervous, because the thought of meeting his family entered my head. I didn't know what to expect. Most likely they would be like him, refined, but I hoped they didn't think of me as white trash – free loading off their son or something.

The car made a sharp turn down a small gravel road that jolted the car slightly. We pulled into a driveway of what looked like a small castle. Darren called it an estate. It towered above us and stood bleak, weather beaten and grey against the blue sky. It was made of large heavy stones, with hundreds of windows at regular intervals. I turned my head from left to right to survey it all.

The car stopped. Our driver was already out of the vehicle,

opening it for Darren to exit.

"That was kinda classy," I thought. Not so up-to-speed with these types of things, I followed him. The driver smiled. I thanked him and he nodded. He went round the back of the car and got our luggage for us.

An older man came out of the front door. He painfully made his way down the large front steps, bowed to Darren and motioned us towards the doors. The man stayed with our luggage and spoke with the driver, as we went in.

Inside I felt like part of some movie. The grand entrance was entirely made of marble and was furnished with dark heavy wood pieces. A small desk was off to the side where a blonde girl stood, silently watching as I looked around. There were rooms off this main hall. It looked like a bar to one side. I couldn't see the rest.

This huge place, the car and driver, the man who shows us around, I wondered if this is how famous people did things.

While I was taking it all in, Darren walked toward the girl and spoke softly with her. The sound of his voice was very calming. A little bell tinkered somewhere and a young man appeared through a doorway and walked towards me.

He must have been roughly my age, but he was taller and obviously well built. He was dressed in a more formal fitted uniform, and he had our suitcases. He stood beside me: he looked sharp, well groomed and appealing. Then there was me – jeans, sweater, most likely haggard looking from the long duration of travel.

Darren turned around and faced the two of us. Holding my breath, jealousy and worry shot through me. Why should Darren spend time with me? I must seem pathetic in this place. Beside this guy, I was pathetic.

Darren walked towards us and stared at me. When he was close enough, he smiled warmly and put his arm across my shoulders. "Come let's go to our room. We can get settled in and then get you some food."

"Alright." I walked with him, but turned my head slightly to see if there had been a reaction from the porter. His jaw looked like it clenched, but he was still maintaining a steady look. I felt a little satisfaction. "Dare, is there a restaurant in here? Or do we have to go out for grub?"

Darren continued up a large staircase, the porter now was in front leading the way to our room. Darren kept his arm in place. "There is dining here. We missed the meal time, but they will accommodate us. I hear they serve a fantastic fish and chips."

He grinned at me. "I knew that was your favourite so I have taken the liberty of having them prepare it for you."

I liked the fact he thought ahead. "Thanks Dare! Did you tell them I'll need lots of tartar sauce though? I'm addicted to the stuff!"

"I will make sure that you have an unlimited supply. Here's our room." We were stopped outside a door in a narrow dim hall. He unlocked the door and gently pushed me into the room first.

It was amazing.

High ceilings, French doors facing outside, a balcony too. Large paintings hung on the walls, and tapestries. Couches and two large overstuffed chairs framed an ornate fireplace that was already lit. On the far end of the room was a large canopy bed, filled with decorative pillows of all shapes and sizes. This place was more high-end than I could have ever afforded.

The door closed. Darren and I just stood there. He had unsure look on his face. "Do you like the room, Markus?" He fiddled with the key in his hand as he spoke. "I hope you like it. This is my favourite one. There is only one bed though. There are no other suites available. You can have the bed, and I can rest on one of the couches if you want," he said sadly as he looked down at the floor.

I smiled. "This room is incredible. It's really awesome." I walked towards the bed to check it out. Pushing down on it, my hands sunk into the feathered softness. "I don't mind sleeping with you so I can stay here!"

His head shot up. Darren looked shocked at my words. I don't think I had ever seen him looked so surprised. It then dawned on me what I had just said.

I corrected myself. "Well. I mean, sharing the bed, with you. I don't have a problem with that. Not that sleeping with you is a problem either. I mean to say, uhmm, that's not what I meant to say. Uhmm ..." My face went beet red, I was clearly putting both feet in my mouth.

Darren smiled and looked down at the floor where he stood, then spoke. "Markus, I know what you meant. Please don't worry yourself about it. Why don't you go and freshen up, have a nice hot shower. I'll have some food brought up here." He seated himself in a chair that faced the fireplace.

"Dare, I hope I didn't offend you or anything? I'm sorry, I didn't mean to!" I stood there for a moment. No response. Sighing, I walked into the bathroom, and closed the door behind me. Obviously, I just made a fool of myself.

The tiles on the floor were frigid. I thought the thick stone walls would keep the inclement weather out, but the cold went right through them. I turned the water on. It was hotter than I would normally have it. The water warmed my bones. Suddenly,

I felt exhausted.

I finished showering and opened the curtain from the tub. On the counter in a neat pile was a pair of fleece jogging pants and a sweat shirt, along with my toiletries bag. Darren must have brought them in for me. Although, I didn't hear him.

I dressed and took a long look in the mirror. Sighing again I grabbed my things and went out the door.

There was a bright light coming from the fireplace mixed with a glow from a lamp that sat on a table between the large wingback chairs. As I made my way towards them I looked out the windows. It was dark out. With no city lights to make the sky brighter, the darkness felt blacker. I didn't want to wander out there by myself.

The floor was cold, so bare feet probably weren't a good idea. I walked up to the fire past the chairs and put my arms out to feel the heat. It warmed the palms of my hands. I turned around to take a seat in one of the arm chairs. I hadn't noticed, but Darren was sitting in one, his hands folded in his lap as usual. He did not say a word, but gazed at the fire.

I flopped in the empty chair and looked at him. "Dare? Whoo hoo? Anyone home?" I waved my hand in front of his face. "Hellooo?"

He refocused his eyes to my face. "Hey. Sorry, I was in thought. How was your shower?"

"Good, lots of hot water. Floors are bloody freezing!"

Darren smiled. "Well, it is winter and it *does* get cold here. Oh, your food is here." He got up out of his chair and went to a little side table by the door. He returned with a tray that he placed on my lap. He removed the shiny silver cover. Piled on a plate sat a large helping of fish and chips, a large bowl of homemade tartar sauce sat along side of it. "Go ahead and eat."

"Awesome, thanks Dare. What about you? Did you eat already?"

He nodded and sat back down in his chair. "Yes, I had a bite while you were in the shower. Please eat Markus before it gets too cold."

I dug my fork into the food and began to eat. "This is good!" The taste was a little different from what I was used to, but it was yummy all the same.

"I'm glad you like it." He paused for a moment. "Are you fine if we spend the evening here? Just in the room? Tomorrow will be a long day I am sure, so I thought maybe a good night's rest would do."

"Sure." I said. "What's the plan for tomorrow? Sight seeing or something?" I took another bite.

"No." He shifted his body a little. "We will go and visit with my family. I figure it best to get that over and done with."

"Oh, uhmm, Would it better if I waited here for you then? I could just order room service and watch T.V." I turned to look for the television set, but there didn't seem to be one.

Darren smirked. "No, I think it would be good for you to meet them. I wanted to introduce you. Besides, there is no T.V. here for you to vegetate in front of."

I had to agree. I think I would have been a little bored in the room all day. "I could always go explore this place, take a walk outside. But, if you really want me to go, then I will." I looked up from my plate at him. "Truth is Darren, I'm kinda nervous about meeting your folks. I might seem really stupid or something to them."

"Markus, I am sure they will like you. But it doesn't matter anyhow, as you are my best friend." Darren faced the fire, then back to me before he continued. "I only ask you one thing, one favour. Please could you not mention your little gift to them?"

"Okay. That's no problem with me. They would think I was a wacko if I did."

He grinned evilly. "You're probably right."

I cracked a smile and threw a light punch at his shoulder from where I sat. "So it's just your parents here then? I know you mentioned you had a sister."

His face went tight with the mention of her. "Chloe will most likely not be there. I hope not at least. I wouldn't want to subject you to her."

Darren then changed the subject and asked me if there were places and tourist attractions I wanted to visit. Seeing as we were here for a short visit, I should pick a few of my top choices. London was the only place I thought of, and of course Stonehenge.

The night seemed to fly by. Before I knew it, the fire was growing dim and I was very sleepy. Yawning, I stretched in my chair. "Alright, I am heading to bed. Are you coming Dare?"

"Ahh ... yes, I suppose. Sleep would be a good thing. I can always just stay on the couch."

I got out of the chair and messed up his short hair with my hand and laughed. "Common Dare, don't be stupid. We can share a bed." I continued to walk, thinking quickly to myself how odd it seemed that we sat so close to the fire, yet Darren's head was frigid, even his hair felt cold. I just shrugged it off.

I threw the spare pillows on the floor, pulled off my sweatshirt, turned the sheets down and climbed into the bed. It was like lying in a bed of feathers, so soft and warm. I wish I could bring this home with me. "Dare, this bed is awesome, I gotta get one!"

He smiled.

Darren then walked over to the opposite side of the bed. He

looked a little nervous, and hesitant. He pulled off his sweater, exposing his muscled bare chest. My cheeks felt flushed. He climbed into the bed, slowly.

We lay facing each other. "Good night Darren. Don't let the monsters bite."

The light of the dying fire reflected on his face, making his smile look somewhat cruel. "I won't bite. Good night Markus."

I closed my eyes.

Sleep quickly took over. Images flashed in my mind ... I was on the plane ... Darren and I were running ... Door after door appeared ... Too many to choose from ... I was falling behind ... Darren reached out his hand but it slipped away ... There was brown grass everywhere as I ran ... I lost my footing ... I couldn't steady myself ... I was struggling to make it up a hill ...

The dream slipped away.

The sheets were thrown down to my waste. Darren's hand slide across my chest, then upward to caress my cheek. He slowly moved his head towards me until we were face to face. His eyes bored into mine, inches away, closer, closer he came. I could feel his breathe on me as he whispered. "It won't hurt, I promise."

He leaned in and kissed me hard.

When he raised himself up and looked down at me, the grin on his face was wicked and evil. He spoke to me, this time harshly. "It's time to finish this buddy!" His words sent me into a panic. My heart pounded, my body tensed, then froze in fear. His lips parted, pearly white fangs now protruded. He lunged towards my throat making me scream out in terror ...

I awoke, bolting up in the bed, gasping for air. It was morning. I must have yelled, as Darren ran to the bed from the opposite side of the room faster than humanly possible. He looked panicked, concern was in his voice as he asked me what was wrong. His hand cupped around my arms almost protectively.

I slowed my breathing a little, finally able to answer. "I'm okay, I'm fine. I just had a nightmare." I swallowed and continued. "It just scared me, You weren't you Darren, I mean you were, but ..."

He sat on the edge of the bed still worried. "Markus, what happened in your dream? Am I giving you nightmares? Did I do something to scare you? Do I scare you? Honestly, I wouldn't do anything to ever ..."

I put my hand up to stop him for continuing. "Dare, no, it was a dream. It was messed up and weird. It was like you were mixed with the crazy guy who attacked me, but then you were a vampire who was going to kill me after you tried to, uhmm ..." I lifted my head to see his face waiting for me to go on. "Well, anyway, just don't worry about it. I guess I was tired and stressed and all this stuff that has happened and the trip and nerves. I guess it all meshed together you know?"

He nodded. "I would never hurt you, Markus. I thought perhaps this trip would be a good thing for you. I wanted you to enjoy yourself and forget about things for awhile."

"I DO! I AM enjoying myself. We just got here yesterday. It was just a dream. So don't sweat it." I forced a smiled.

The nightmare happened to me. Why was I the one who was trying to reassure Darren? He was the one person who was always in control, always confident.

"So?" I questioned. "What time do we go to see your family? Oh, and Dare, I have something else I want to ask you. It's really important, but I think you can handle it."

He sat waiting for me to continue. If it was possible for the colour to drain from him, it did.

"Can we get breakfast now? I'm super hungry and ..."

WHOOMP.

A pillow walloped me in the side of the head.

Darren grinned. He swung the pillow again. I was ready this time, I wasn't about to let him win this one. I grabbed my pillow and flung it at him. The fight began, both of us on the bed and armed. The air was filled with feathers as we wrestled each other. I felt like a ten year old boy. It was childish, but we were having fun. I gave in as I wasn't able to force Darren off the bed. He was amused and happy being the winner.

We ordered breakfast for me as Darren had eaten before I woke. When it arrived I was careful not to open the door wide as I didn't want the staff to notice the mess in the room and the explosion of pillows. I ate while Darren showered. Then it was mine turn to get ready. By the time I was done in the bathroom and dressed it was almost two p.m. Where did the start of the day go?

We went downstairs to the main entrance. Darren went to the front desk again, I guessed maybe to apologise for the damages to our room. The thought made me chuckle. When he came back we went outside to where our same car and driver waited with the door open. Darren with his sunglasses on, even in the drizzle and overcast weather, hurried into the vehicle.

There were no words spoken to our chauffer. He already seemed to know where we were going. Since it was light out, I could see the landscape better now. Green rolling hills and trees. Farm fields, and little cottages. It was all the same scene as we made our way.

At last we arrive at our destination. A country palace. It was massive. Other cars were out front. Two men came to open both of our doors as we pulled to a stop. Silent again, we walked to the grand entrance. The doors opened.

Inside, the mega rich sat at little tables here and there talking amongst themselves. Puffs of smoke and clinking of glasses were everywhere I looked. An older man came forward to us, he must have known or expected Darren, as he greeted and called him young Sir Von Land, and ushered us forward to a room off the side of the main area. A large door was opened. The man was pulling it closed, when I heard my watch beep. Outside a car door slammed and a dog barked. Inside a bottle fell to the floor and smashed, someone yelled and I felt a cold chill of wind.

Click.

The door closed.

I turned and for the first time I laid eyes on the devil herself.

Chloe Von Land did not need introduction. Her long, straight black hair was a contrast to her delicate pale skin. Beautiful she was, breath taking, innocent looking, the picture-perfect maiden, damsel in distress. With one small difference. Her eyes, her dark eyes held a certain cruelty, a wickedness.

She laid seductively on a chez lounge in the private room. A fluffy black cat with large green eyes draped itself across her. It purred loudly as she caressed it. The cat looked exactly like the one back in Boston. Strange. But there was no way it was the same one.

Chloe smiled at us, delicately collected herself and rose. I could tell Darren was very close to me. His coolness almost touching me. Closer still she walked towards us. Coming to a stop in front of us, she raised her hand palm down and spoke in a soft manner similar to Darren. The only difference being she spoke with a subtle

French accent.

"I am Chloe Von Land. And you would be?"

I took her hand and shook it assuming that was what she wanted.

"I'm, uhmm Markus Benson. Pleasure to meet you finally."

She smiled and then turned to embrace her brother. She spoke as they touched. "My dear brother, it has been too long. It is always nice to know that I am in your thoughts. Speaking well of me of course to your ... How you say? Your friend?" She smiled at him in a devilish way, and said something else to him in French.

He glared at her. "Of course, I always speak of you in a good way, my dear sister. How have you been? Well, I assume?"

"Yes, brother, of course. I am always well. Come sit, let us have a drink."

She motioned to a low table that faced outside towards the gardens.

Darren held her chair for her, and then gestured for me to sit on his other side, away from his sister. He sat towards her and spoke. "Where are mother and father? I assumed they would be here."

She laughed a little before answering. "No, they are not here now. They have decided to stay on where they are a little longer. The left a message for us, giving us their best wishes for the year. They will see us again another time."

Darren looked irritated. "So, just you and I then?"

"Yes, my brother." She smirked, then faced me. "Markus is it?"

"Yes." I nodded.

"Tell, me." She twisted a piece of hair in her little fingers. "How do you know my brother?"

"Uhmm, well I live in Boston, so we met there. What about you? Where do you live?"

She leaned her head to the side a little then answered with her soft French voice. "I have spent most of my life in France. I still reside there. I have no use for the west. All culture and fashion and life is over here. Only my dear brother went across to new lands."

"Oh, really?" I leaned forward a little, as that was not something I had known. "I guess your parents wanted him to have a different education or something?" I thought it was a good question.

Chloe tilted her head back and let out a evil peel of laughter. Darren gave her a nasty look. She then glowered back and answered my question. "No, my simple friend. My brother was not sent. He ran away there. Did he never tell you? Darren?" She scolded him then turned back to me. "He went there to hide from his shame. He was to blame for the death of my true love you know. Did he never tell you of that?"

She leaned back in her chair and smiled. Darren sat his hands folded in his lap as usual, this time his knuckles were white with rage. My mouth dropped. I hadn't expected that so I didn't know how to respond. Chloe on the other hand had more to say. "Is history going to repeat itself Darren? Except this time, maybe you will lose me? Is this the reason for your friend being here? Hmmm? Tell me brother dear?"

Again another solitary comment in French that I did not understand.

Darren stood up furious. "Watch your mouth sister. You are not the most wholesome creature!"

Her face contorted for a moment, then she regained her composure. "Brother, why don't you fetch poor Markus here a drink. We should make this short visit civil, you don't want him to think poorly of us do you?" Her eyes flashed a very hard look, almost a warning.

Darren got out of his chair. I too started to rise, but he caught my shoulder and told me he'd be back momentarily. There I sat, facing Chloe. She held the smile on her face. Finally she looked away, then reached for a silver case that sat on the table. She popped it open and produced a cigarette. She lit it and inhaled deeply. Feigned shock and apology now came from her. "Markus, I am so very sorry, how very rude of me. Would you care for a cigarette?"

"No thank you." I said shaking my head at the same time. Then I turned to take in the view of the garden.

"There are worse things that could kill you." She responded. "But, eventually you will figure that out."

I had no clue what she meant by that, but I could see now why Darren had no use for her. She was not a nice person at all. I hoped Darren would return soon, because I really didn't want to be alone with her. I just wanted to leave.

The door clicked. I felt relief, but that quickly vanished when I heard Chloe clap her hands together in excitement. "There he is!" She jumped out of her chair and ran over to the sunglass clad stranger who now stood in the room. She threw her arms around him and kissed him – or I should say ravaged him.

Slightly embarrassed I turned away. They were having a moment, so I figured it was best to put my attention elsewhere. The garden was a good choice, the odd person strolled by, so I would concentrate on that.

A moment or two later the couple returned to the table. The man held out the chair for Chloe, and then came my way. He held out his hand. "Hey. I'm Alex." There was no foreign accent. He was clearly from North America.

I shook his cold hand and looked up at his face. "I'm Markus. Nice to meet you."

He had a pale complexion and a wide smile. There was a familiarity about him.

He took the seat on the right of Chloe, leaving Darren's chair empty. They faced each other and smiled, joining hands. I felt like telling them to rent a room, but I was trying to be on my best behaviour. Instead I tried to make small talk. "So, where did you two meet?"

Alex responded. "I was on business in Paris when I met Chloe. My heart was stopped by this beauty, so I am hers forever." He kissed her hand.

I wanted to roll my eyes, but figured keeping them talking might keep them off each other. "So, uhmm, what do you do? Like, your business, what is it?"

"Oh, acquisitions. I am a procurer of sorts. And what is it you do Markus?" He faced me now, his dark glasses still hiding his eyes. It sent a chill down my spine.

"I, uhmm, I work in a bookshop in Boston." I felt stupid saying it. Almost like I was a child at an all-adult table, trying to act grown up.

Alex nodded. He kissed Chloe's hand again, then brought his attention back to me. "You live in Boston then right? Dangerous place huh?" A smirk settled on his pale face. "You really need to be careful there. Makes sure you pay attention not to get lost in some scary dark street."

Why did it seem these people were intent on making me feel really uncomfortable? I wanted Darren back in the room now. I didn't like these two strangers and I wanted to go. I felt a surge in my stomach and felt the pull as I wished for Darren to come through the door of the room.

The door swung opened and there was my saviour Darren. His face was livid. He stormed into the room and slammed a glass down hard in front of me. It spilled a little on the table. I mumbled my thanks and took a sip. It was cola. I drank more as Darren seated himself.

Immediately, he noticed Alex. Without even introducing himself, Darren turned on

his sister. He pointed his finger at Alex. "Who is this? Chloe who is your pet?"

She smiled sweetly. "My dear brother, this is my love, Alex. We met recently, he is on business in London. I wanted him to meet the family. Is that wrong of me?"

Darren clenched his jaw. "No, I suppose it is not."

She continued. "He is special to me. Just like I have noticed, Markus is special. He has a certain charm about him, a magical quality even. Don't you think brother?" She mumbled something in French.

Her smile faded and her face hardened.

Darren stood up and motioned for me to do the same. He grabbed the back of my shirt and yanked me out my chair. "We take our leave now sister. Until later."

He went to her and kissed her on the cheek. She did not respond, but sat cold in her chair. I didn't know if I should do the same, so I just waved and said goodbye and it was nice to meet them both.

Alex smiled at me. He put his hand up to wave and spoke one last time to me. "Nice to see you, until later." The smiled changed to an evil grin as he said his last word: "*Buddy.*"

I froze.

Darren pulled at me and forced me to move out of the room. We hurried out of the building. I hadn't noticed any details as we left, it was like a bad dream. I was lost in my own thoughts.

We were in the car again. The English countryside streamed by as I focused on reality. Darren's head faced the window, his hands on his knees, white knuckles still. I wondered if he knew? Did he realize how that word had bothered me. Was it coincidence that Alex used the same nickname? Or was Darren's fury directed at me for willing him into the room, or was it just anger at his sister?

I gazed out of my window. I didn't want to say anything to him that would push him over the edge. I just kept quiet. I felt the fear starting to build more inside. How odd it was to sit so close to the one person who saved me, and had known what I went through, yet I couldn't tell him about what I thought right now. How I knew I was going to die.

We pulled into the drive where we were staying. When the car stopped at the front entrance Darren turned to me, still angry. "Wait here in the car. Don't leave it. I will be back in 10 minutes. Do you understand me Markus?"

I could barely speak. "Yah. Sure." It was all I could voice.

Darren got out and slammed the door shut. The driver had remained in his seat with the engine still running. I didn't know what to do. I could tell this vacation was over. Should I get out and ask for another car and take myself to the airport? I didn't have my ticket or my passport with me. My things were up in the room.

Maybe that is what Darren was doing. Packing all my stuff up so he could send me home. I did the one thing he asked me not to do, willing him in the room. But he had said not to 'tell' his family about my little thing, but I was certain he also meant not to use it around them as well.

Ten minutes later Darren walked down the steps carrying two

suitcases. The trunk of our car popped open and he dumped the luggage in. He climbed into the car telling the driver "London." Then he faced me. "Markus?"

"Yes?" I didn't know what he wanted to say.

He grabbed my hand. "I will not let anything happen to you! Nothing. I will keep you safe."

He straightened himself in his seat and said nothing more. The conversation was done. But he refused to let go of my hand. He held it with a firm grip. I felt some relief and relaxed a little.

The drive went for a long time. I fell asleep at some point, waking only to the noise of traffic around us. The city lights were bright, but the dark tint of the glass muted it all. We twisted and turned through the crowded streets. I felt nauseous, we needed to stop the car soon, I couldn't take much more of this closed-in space.

The car stopped outside of a brightly lit grand hotel. The Hotel Grosvenor Kensington. It was massive.

Porters came to open the doors. They took our bags and escorted us into the lobby. Darren kept his hand protectively across my back. It was like having a human shield blocking me from the oncoming horror.

We got our keys and went to our room. Darren said we should go out for something to eat, because I had been cooped up in rooms too much lately. It would have been fine with me if we had stayed in. I was scared to go outside.

The night was teaming with life as we walked down Pelham Street. It was cold and damp as the people of this city made their way to their destinations. Talking and laughter seemed all around us, but we weren't a part of it. Fear was getting the best of me now. Darren noticed that too.

"Markus? Hey, are you alright?" He placed his arm around my shoulder. "I think you must be hungry. It's way past your feeding time!" He attempted humour and smiled.

I tried to do the same back but it didn't happen. There were two things on my mind. I needed to speak them now. "Darren? Can I ask you something?"

"Yes, of course. What?"

"I know you asked me not to say anything about my gift at making certain things happen, to your family. But, are you mad because I made you come back into the room? It was only because they were scaring me, and I really wanted to get out of there. I didn't know where you were."

He stopped, brushed something out of my hair and faced me. "Markus, I was ...Yes, I was angry that you did that. You have no idea how it feels! I can resist it, but it's like a constant tugging. I was speaking with a staff about my parents' message, when I felt the sensation of you pulling at me, mixed with feeling your stress and desperation of wanting me there. I had no choice but to go to you."

He looked up at the sky, squinting a little with the drizzle that fell. His eyes returned to mine as he continued. "I knew my sister had said or did something to you, so most of the frustration was to be directed at her. And then when I saw *him* there ..." His voice trailed off.

"Darren? Uhmm, what happened to your sister's boyfriend? The one that died I mean? She said you ... well, it was your fault? Was that true?"

There was remorse on his face as it tightened. "Yes." He whispered between clenched teeth. "Yes, it was my fault. Markus. I didn't know!" He bowed his head. "I didn't know it would happen, now

I have to live with that guilt forever."

"What happened? Please tell me. Dare?" I couldn't take my eyes off him.

He took a breathe and started. "I was in love... one other time. Either it was the blindness of the first time or my sheer stupidity and innocence. I brought my lover into my life and made him a part of my family. Apparently, that had been his goal all along. I had no idea. Now armed with power and great hunger, my lover had no use for me and tried to take everything possible, anything he wanted and craved.

Chloe's love had seen this from the beginning. He had warned me but I ignored him. He took it upon himself to go confront my lover and put an end to his seemingly unstoppable path of destruction. The end result... they both died in the struggle. I never found out what happened exactly. My parents dealt with it and refused to ever speak of it again." He folded his arms across his chest. "So, now I live with that guilt and the hatred my sister has for me. I cannot undo that. I was foolish as my sister has reminded me. I do not deserve to be happy ever again."

The two of us stood still in the street. There seemed to be no sound. The cold drizzle fell silently. It was the first time Darren had ever spoke openly about his choice of love. I had always known and it made no difference to me, it was just surprising to hear him say it was all. I stepped closer to him.

"Hey, Dare. I don't think you did anything wrong. How were you to know? It's all a part of life right? I think you need to stop blaming yourself!" I was the one now putting my arm over his shoulder. "Come on, I'm hungry. We better get something to eat before I turn into a crazy monster."

We started to walk, he turned his head and smiled weakly. "Okay. Thank you Markus."

"No worries. I'm always here to listen. Now, since you know where we are, why don't you lead the way. Maybe somewhere not too far because it feels like it's starting to rain harder."

"Alright." Darren agreed. "There is a place just a couple streets over that I have been to before. I'm sure you'll like it. You're right though, it is starting to pour."

We quickened our pace and headed down the street towards the pub.

We were soaked by the time we got there, but it didn't matter as inside it was warm and dry. We found seats, sat back and relaxed.

It seemed like hours later we left. Full of food and beer, I was in my happy place. Darren declined food as his stomach was bothering him, apparently from the upset of the days events. Oh well, at least he drank with me. For once I managed to not drink myself silly. There was so much I wanted to see and do. Sporting a hangover would ruin that, so I paced myself.

We left the pub with the intent to return to our hotel, but then decided a stroll down Old Brompton Road. The rain subsided and was drizzle again. I came to the conclusion that I still preferred the snow. We were caught up in our idle chit chat and banter as we walked, wandering past many little storefronts, cafes, and restaurants. It was all so different than the streets of my Boston home.

We turned a corner and walked down a path of steps that lead to a narrow street. It was fun how everything seemed to interconnect, almost like a well put together puzzle. Our footsteps echoed off the walls of the buildings as we went. Amazing how silent it could all be. There weren't any other people around. Just Darren and I. I hoped he knew how to get back to the hotel. I had no idea where we were.

The damp chill started to set in. I started to shake a little. It triggered a memory of a night not too long ago where I walked cold, alone and lost. It seemed so surreal. Then I heard it.

"Tap. Tap. Tap."

I looked to Darren. "Did you hear that?" My breathing became faster.

"The tapping? Yes, but I wasn't paying attention to it. I started to hear it awhile ago, but it seemed like nothing. Why?" He raised his eyebrow as my reaction to the noise interested him.

I continued walking. "Nothing. It just creeped me out."

The noise came again. This time a little louder, almost intentionally louder. "TAP. TAP. TAP."

I turned my head quickly to search for the origin of the noise, but there was nothing. "Doesn't that creep you out? It does me!" I was panicking now. "I wish I knew where it was coming from."

The shudder of my insides.

Must be the damp I thought.

Then came another "Tap. Tap. Tap." I could see a figure in the distance with a white baseball cap leaning against the wall up ahead. He had something in his hand which must have been the source of the mysterious tapping.

I looked closer at the stranger. He was hard to miss with a white hooded sweater and dark glasses. Suddenly my knees felt weak and I started to shake. Darren stopped walking. He shocked me as he pushed me up against a wall that was to our side.

He turned around and pressed his back up against me and spread his arms out as if to shield me. I heard the "Tap. Tap. Tap."

again. It was very close. Then came laughter, followed by a familiar voice. "Hey, Buddy. So good to see you again." It was Alex.

Darren growled. "How dare you bother us. What the hell do you want you piece of filth?"

Alex snickered, then responded. "Ha, you think you are better than me? That's the one thing I hate about your sister. I guess it's genetic. You and her both think you're so much better than the rest of us. Well guess again. Because you're not! But, I should thank her for dragging me out to this bore of a city. Look at my good fortune of being lucky enough to find that whimpering fool again. Imagine my surprise to be half way around the world and run into my little unfinished play date. I guess it was meant to be."

Alex bent forward, as if ready to strike. There was a real danger about him, something very scary. He lifted his face a little and his dark glasses reflected the light – as did his fangs.

"Oh god." I stared in horror. Darren and I were done for, there was no way out for us. My mind flashed to Chloe. I was sure Alex must have killed her before coming for us. We were about to suffer the same fate.

Alex shifted toward us slowly. Darren stepped forward to meet him. Was he mad? What did he think he was doing? How on earth could he take on a monster?

Like an answer to my question, the battle began.

Alex appeared suddenly in front of Darren and they locked arms. They pushed against each other, snarls and shouts echoed in the lane way. Darren was smacked into the wall. I moved out of the way just in time to escape being crushed. Darren pushed forward at Alex with more force and sent him flying backwards to the ground.

Darren pounced on Alex. It was like he thrust himself up into the air and slammed down into his rival. I heard something crunch and Alex let out a howl of rage. Again Darren jumped up and crushed into Alex. His third attempt missed. Alex rolled out of the way. The cobblestones took Darren's full force and crumbled beneath it. I had never known someone so powerful that they could crush stone.

Alex was on his feet again. The beating he had already taken didn't slow him down. He was back at Darren in a flash, arms locked again. A second later, Darren came crashing to the ground, Alex reappeared beside him and kicked at him with all his force. His foot caught Darren and sent him flying into a wall, but Darren bounded up it and came rushing down from twenty feet above onto Alex. Then came the sound of snapping. Alex screamed, as did I. Darren grabbed both of Alex's arms, he shook them quick and violently breaking both of them in that instant. He began to twist them and turn them as if to rip them out of their sockets. I stood and gasped in horror.

Darren spun round at me. The angry rage on his face disappeared and was replaced by his immediate realization that I was still present during this dreadful event. Alex took the brief moment and ran. He bolted to the wall across the street and ran up it. One of his arms apparently still had some use.

I stared after him. This wasn't right, none of this fight was right. It made no sense.

I didn't grasp the sheer impossibility of what had occurred until Darren walked up to me, concern for me now evident in his features – along with a set of white fangs. I was in disbelief. My heart fluttered and pounded hard. It seemed night closed in on me in an instant and the world disappeared before my eyes. I felt my body falling, then nothing.

It must have been hours later when I finally came to. I slowly opened my eyes to the filtered morning sun that came through the curtains in our hotel room. I slowly lifted myself up so that I was sitting in the bed. I had no idea how I had got back to the hotel. I guess Darren must have dragged me.

Then the sense of fear came flooding back, where was Darren? What did he want, why was he my friend? Was he going to kill me? No, I had a feeling he did not want to hurt me at all. He was the one who always seemed to be there for me and keep the danger away.

I glanced around the room, no one else was there. The curtains were drawn so thin lines of the sunlight could filter through. But I was alone and it was quiet. I was never one for quietness, especially in a room. The space was closing in. I decided to get out of bed and open up the heavy curtains to let in more of the morning. As I did, the sun faded behind a thick cover of clouds. This place felt a little gloomy. Oh well, I thought. I left the sheers closed so I still had some privacy.

I wandered around the room, opening the little drawers here and there, looking at some of the details of the decorations so that I could keep occupied. I was waiting for something, but I didn't know what. Maybe for Darren? Last night's disaster deserved a discussion. I felt I was owed that much. Hopefully, Darren would be back soon so we could talk about it.

Someone knocked on the door. A porter with a cart – apparently my breakfast. He wheeled it in the room, then left. I stared at the order I never placed. I suppose I knew someone who would have been thoughtful enough to have taken care of this for me.

The food was really good, but I rushed through my breakfast so

I could get showered and dressed. I wanted to be ready when Darren got back.

I thought over the last night's events as I got ready, then back to the first meeting of Alex in Boston. It all clicked, the things my mind shut away – Darren being crushed into a wall and being unscathed – it all made sense now. I had lived through two vampire fights centered around me. My stomach turned. Waves of nausea. I dropped down on the cold bathroom floor cradling myself. They are real. Vampires. They really do exist. I had always wanted to see it since I was a child. Back in Ms. Havish's library, thinking about when I might meet a real vampire and wishing one day to become one. And now, here I was, years later and half a world away, being chased, hunted down by one, who didn't want to make me the same as him, but to kill me for sport. On the other hand, another vampire who was my friend, protecting and saving me each time. My head felt like it would explode. Vampires are real ...

I wondered if Darren would ever want to make me like him? I wasn't sure that he would. Maybe once we talked about everything. I slowly stood up, my legs felt weak and shaky. I had to finish getting myself put together.

I flipped on the T.V. to pass the time while I waited. Hopefully, Darren wouldn't be gone too much longer. Yet, I was nervous to see him again. Unsure of his intent.

I finally gave up on T.V. It had been a few hours now. I needed air. I needed to get out of this room. I guessed I would be spending this day on my own.

I grabbed my coat and the room key from a side table. There was a wad of money sitting beside it. Darren's, I borrowed it. He wouldn't mind. I would pay him back. Besides, he couldn't expect me to sit around all day doing nothing and have no money to go out. He was the one who dragged me here. Anger started to build in me. Why was I being left alone?

Frustrated, I left the room. I was determined to go and have a good day, go explore, enjoy my own company. I walked down the hallway and bounded down the main stairs and stopped only to grab a map that was available at the front desk. With that, I exited through the front doors and made my way into the afternoon.

The sun broke through every now and then as I walked. It was damp and cold, but it felt good to be out of the confines of four walls. I stopped and grabbed a coffee to go. I had only had one with breakfast, so I was in need of more caffeine.

The streets were busy and teaming with life. I felt safe in public view. Anytime the crowd lessened, I changed direction to find a busier area. I made the day about exploring. I decided to wander through South Kensington. There were so many shops and restaurants. I would stop and gawk at the old world charm. Somehow, I made my way to Knightsbridge, Sloan Street. I definitely was out of place. The people that passed by me had money – and lots of it. Designer clothes and designer shops dotted the streets. I thought it best to make my way back towards the hotel. Besides, I wanted to be back before nightfall.

I had used a pen and traced my route on the map so I was able to find my way back. I was thankful I had done this, because I had gotten so caught up in my exploration I realized that the sun was setting. I picked up my pace and made my way back.

It was dark out now, a couple of hours had passed by the time I had made the long walk back. I only stopped along the way for another coffee to keep warm. The feeling of fear of the dark wasn't as bad. My route had been filled with crowds of people in the day, and at night the faces were different but the amount of people was unchanged. There was security in that fact. Besides, Alex had both his arms broken by Darren, so I was sure I would be fine tonight.

The hotel lobby was busy as I entered. All the lamps were lit and added to the warm glow. It reminded me of something out of a movie from the old-days, and here I was a part of it. I suddenly realized how wet I was as the warmth of the hotel hit me. Hours of walking in the damp and drizzle. I was wet through and through.

I went to my room and was glad to be back. The lamps were on and the bed had been turned down. "What service." I thought. As I put down the bags from my day of shopping on a nearby chair, I realized how many little things I had bought. I didn't remember having that much money, but I hadn't counted the little pile I borrowed, so I couldn't be sure.

I pulled off my coat and shoes. It was like stripping away ten pounds. They weighed so much more with the wet. Then my jeans and sweater, they were surprisingly damp too. I walked over to the couch and sat down, grabbing the room service menu from the side table.

I placed my order and waited. Had Darren ever come back to the room? Would he really leave me here all alone? Force me to make my way back to Boston by myself?

The thought of Claire, in the bookstore, trying out some magic tricks from her new little book popped in my head. I was certain she would say, "I told you so!" if I told her about this adventure, the vampire incident and Darren being one of them. That fact would add to the list of reasons why she didn't like Darren. But maybe she already knew, maybe one of her little fairies told her. I laughed out loud at the though of a little gnome whispering into her ear, having to push one of the butterfly clips out of the way.

A knock at the door. The food service at the hotel was really quick. I was starving so it was well timed. I went to the door and opened it wide.

There stood Darren.

His usually well-kept appearance was gone. He was soaked to the bone. His clothes looked filthy and his face, paler than usual, had misery written all over it. I automatically reached forward and pulled him into the room and closed the door. He stood there not saying anything. So I did.

"What the hell Darren? Where have you been? No call, no note, no message to tell me anything!" I was getting angry and clenched my fists. " SO where were you huh?"

He looked at me and then wordlessly shrugged his shoulders in a response.

I wasn't about to let that be his response. "Darren, I think you owe me an explanation! Why didn't you tell me about you? Why didn't you ever tell me about Alex? Then I wake up this morning, no one in sight, no idea if you took off back to Boston and left me here! I had no money, nothing. I had to borrow money I found of yours so I could get food!" I was feeling hot, my temper raging.

He finally spoke. "Markus, I would not have left you here. I ...I just needed time to think." He sat down on a chair, then continued. "I didn't know if you would want me around. Your face last night, it was so scared. I was afraid you would never want me around anymore."

"Darren, I was shocked last night. Think about it, I had no clue about you and Alex, then you guys are going at each other with super human strength – all I see and hear are bones being crushed and snapped. Then you turned around and stared at me like you're ready to tear me into shreds. Of course I was scared. I probably shit my pants."

Darren flashed a quick grin before he responded. "No, you didn't do that. But seriously Markus. I wanted to tell you, but I didn't know how you would take it. How could I tell you a secret like that without you thinking I am crazy or scaring you. What if you tell people about me. You are my best friend. I couldn't loose that. I didn't want to scare you away."

He got off the chair and began to pace the room. I was sure he didn't notice – but I did – his pacing was faster than I could watch. He was back and forth across the room in mere seconds. It was a little unnerving.

He stopped abruptly.

"Markus, tomorrow we are going home."

"WHAT?" Why would he want to do that?

Darren stood closer to me now and answered. "You know what Alex is. He will heal in enough time and then come here looking for you. It's not safe here anymore. We'll go home, then I can figure out how to keep you safe."

"But, our trip? I wanted to show you a couple of places I found today. They were so cool, I thought you'd really like them."

"No, we must leave tomorrow. Perhaps another time we can return and you can show me."

With that he turned and walked away. He went to the closet and began to pull some dry clothes out for himself. He started to undress and remove the wet clothes, I just watched. I was unsure what just happened. He was upset, but now he was decided and formal.

It was driving me crazy, his mood swings.

My thoughts were interrupted with a knock at the door. Who would that be? I yanked the door open. "What?" The man sent to the room with my dinner was slightly shocked, most likely from the way I answered the door and the fact I was wearing only my underwear. Mortified, I thanked him, took my meal and quickly shut the door.

I carried my food to the couch and sat. It smelled good, but my hunger had passed. I wasn't in the mood to eat, so I sat there and stared blank at the wall.

Darren wearing nothing but a towel wrapped around his waste came over towards me. He looked down and noticed the meal sitting, being untouched.

"Markus, please eat. I'm sure it will be to your liking. Besides, you don't want to waste it." He looked from the food to my face before continuing. "I am going to take a shower now. I won't be long. Please don't answer the door to anyone. And come get me if you need anything."

He walked away.

I sat for a moment, then decided to eat. Thoughts of this short lived trip ran through my brain. It was kind of a whirlwind of events. I wasn't looking forward to the plane ride home, it would be long and uncomfortable. The plane made me feel even more clostrophobic. Oh well, it was the only way we could go home. Home? Would I even be able to go back there to my little apartment? Would Alex hunt me down? Would Darren even let me go back? Would I now be Darren's prisoner? With Alex around I would be dead. With Darren I would be held captive it seemed, to keep me safe. It wasn't a bad thing necessarily. But I knew I would only be able to take so much, especially if he made me stay inside all the time.

I turned back to the T.V. for comfort and distraction.

Darren came out all cleaned up in his sweatpants and sat beside me on the couch. We didn't say anything. I looked at him for a moment. It was odd to think he was not human. Every part of him looked it, but I supposed that was the difference, he was perfect, and I – the real human – was not. One day I would have to get him to tell me about being a vampire. For now, I went back to watching the mind numbing program.

CHAPTER SEVEN

ENLIGHTENED

The weeks that followed our return to Boston were aggravating. I was cooped up in my apartment of all places. Darren explained if Alex was to return to find us, he knew that Darren would not have let me return here, so in fact it was the safest place to be for us right now.

Finally, I put my foot down. I needed money to pay rent, so I had to go to work. Marge, the land lady, had already banged on my door, dressed in her shiny pink tracksuit, holding out her hand expecting money to be placed in it. Fortunately, I had some to give her but asked for an extension for the rest. Darren said he would give me the money, but I refused. I didn't want to be dependant on him.

I was thankful of my shifts at the bookstore. It gave me some time to myself. I enjoyed Darren's company, but his constant vigilance drove me crazy. Once it was dark he stood at the window staring out for hours. Occasionally, he would come into my room and sit on the bed while I slept. I would wake and he would leave. He seemed to be in a depression. He barely talked to me, or answered my questions. I was sure he would eventually snap out of it.

Winter was bleak. There was snow, too much, and it was so cold. I craved the warmth of the sun, but I knew it was still months away until the warmer weather. I hadn't had any shifts with Claire since my return. It was a slow time for the shop, so there wasn't the need for two of us at one time. Finally today, we would be working together.

It was good to see her and the butterflies stuck in her hair. When I went behind the counter to put my bag and coat down Claire gave me a big hug. "I missed you soo much Markus! I never get to see you anymore! It's so unfair. I complained to Dan about our shifts, so he fixed it now. I hope you don't mind?" She smiled widely at me.

"I don't mind at all. It's nice to have a cheerful person around."

"What do you mean? Is Darren making you miserable? I know it's him. He has such a bad aura you know. I think he attracts negativity. Honestly, you should keep away from him, or things will start happening to you." She stood with her hands on her hips. She continued talking in her manner-of-fact tone. "Oh, I have been practising with all those spells in that book I showed you. They all work. It's so great you know. I even tried making some up of my very own. They work too. You should try it.

"Well, uhmm, I don't know Claire." I shrugged. "That magic stuff seems like it could be a little dangerous don't you think? I mean one wrong word and something could go very badly."

"Oh Markus, you worry too much! The fairies would tell me if there was any danger. Besides, it's good to practice, that way you can control your magic better. Nothing worse than an out of control witch you know."

I laughed. It was such a good feeling. Claire chuckled too. She had a good point though. If I practiced, then I would be better at my control. Practise makes perfect was the saying after all.

The rest of the day past with Claire telling me all about her little spells and how it all turned out. I wasn't sure I believed it all, but I was happy for her. She was so proud of her accomplishments. It was the best day I had in the past while.

Darren met me after work across the street. Apparently, I needed a chaperone so I would make it home in one piece. Claire glared at him and left without a word. It would have been good if they had liked each other. But for some reason Claire had never liked him after the car accident I predicted. Maybe it was due to the fact Darren was teaching me how to control my will and not her.

Darren said nothing to me as I walked up to him. He looked around quickly and we began walking home. The growing silence between us was getting worse and I wasn't liking it. I wanted to know what his problem was. It was time for a little talk.

We arrive home to the smell of food cooking. Darren had prepared a meal for me, which was surprising. The smell of roast beef and potatoes filled my nostrils. It was making me famished. I figured it was Darren's attempt at making up. I had to admit. It worked. How could I possibly be angry with someone who made me a meal like this?

"Thanks Dare. You shouldn't have done this, I mean it smells great and I can't wait to eat, but it was a lot of work to make all that for just one person."

He opened the oven and pulled out the roasting pan with his bare hands. I didn't even own a roasting pan. I wondered where it came from. He set it down on the stove top and began to carve a piece.

He brought me a plate of a large chunk of roast and potatoes covered in a thick dark gravy. I looked up at him. "Awesome, thanks. Oh man this smells so good."

He handed me utensils, and I began to devour the food. I finished it quickly, so I got up and dished out another plateful. Darren walked out of the kitchen. I sat back down and began to eat round two. It took awhile for me to notice that Darren had quietly left my apartment. He had never done this since we had come back from our trip, so I knew this was different.

I started to panic. It was a really long time since I had been alone. Was it safe for me now? Maybe Alex wasn't coming back? I wasn't sure why he was gone, but I had hoped it wasn't for long. It was amazing how much a part of my life Darren had become, so I hated the thought that he had left.

I sat alone for a long time in my kitchen. Finally sleep was getting the best of me, so I went into my room and closed the door. The room was cool and dark. I curled up in a ball and fell asleep. My old nightmare of being torn at by a monster in my apartment returned.

The morning came fast. I could see the light through the gap under my door. I knew Darren was not there, because it just felt different. I got up to get ready for work, wondering if it was all a bad dream. I wasn't sure what was happening, but there wasn't anyone who I could ask.

Once again Claire was working the same shift as me, so it was good to have her around. She noticed that something wasn't right and asked what happened. I didn't tell her. It was personal to me. I didn't know why, but I didn't want to tell her – or admit – that Darren was gone.

After many coffees and pointless conversations, I started to feel a little better. I was amazed at how having Claire around made that happen. It made me almost forget my worries. It was bizarre, maybe she put a spell on me. I chuckled to myself.

It was dark out already. The day had flown by quickly. Claire went to the front door to lock it and flip the closed sign over. When she turned around she was grinning widely.

I was curious. "What's up Claire?"

"Ohh, well, I just had the most amazing idea. Do you have plans tonight Markus? Oh, I forgot, of course you don't. I am going to order us pizza and then we are going to have some fun!" She skipped to the back of the store.

Sometimes Claire made no sense at all. Although, I think she just wanted to keep me company for awhile so I didn't get depressed. It was odd though, because I never mentioned anything about Darren not being around. I just shrugged it off.

Claire returned to the front of the store with her purse in hand. She walked past me and went to the front door. She turned just before unlocking it. "Markus, you like veggies right?"

I nodded. "Yeah, sure I do."

"Okay, I will be right back then, don't go anywhere. Oh we are going to have fun, fun, fun!" Claire giggled and then left the store.

I stood at the front counter for a few minutes more thinking random thoughts before I sat in one of the comfy chairs. It was nice to just relax, especially somewhere that wasn't home. Nothing here reminded me so much of Darren, so it was easy to think.

Eventually Claire came back carrying a pizza. It smelled good. I noticed that her other hand held a large brown paper bag.

She winked and lifted the bag a little. "Refreshments, we must have that you know."

I laughed. "Of course."

"Well, why don't we go upstairs and sit on the couches. People will just stare at us if we sit here. Come on Markus."

I followed her.

We settled in on the big couch. Almost like magic, Claire pulled two glasses out of nowhere and uncorked the large bottle of wine she had bought. She poured us each a glass. We clinked our glasses together and drank them down. It was really good. Most likely cheap, but good. She poured us another glass.

We sat, ate and drank. It seemed the wine was unending and I was getting tipsy. Claire was rambling on about some myths about magic. Things I had already known due to all that time reading the books in Ms. Havish's library.

Then she said something that caught my attention. "So, there is this one story I heard a long, long time ago, when I was a little girl. My mother told me it. She said her mom told her and her mom told her. You know like a family thing passed down the generations." Claire shifted a little, poured herself and I another glass of wine and continued.

"A young, beautiful and powerful witch lived hundreds of years ago. She was known to be fair, gentle and peaceful. She lived on her own in a little white cottage that was at the ocean. The locals would come and bring her gifts and food in return for her help."

I laughed a little and cut Claire off with my question. "What type of help? Was she a prostitute? I bet she was popular. No wonder she could afford to live at the beach."

That was hilarious, my wine spilt as I rolled onto the floor in drunken hysterics. Claire could not help finding humour in my stupid interruption. We giggled for a while longer, then finally we're able to pull it together. I sat quietly and let Claire continue with her story.

"So ... before I was interrupted. Uh hmm." She pointed her finger at me then went on.

"The young witch would help these poor people out. She cured the ill, helped ease the pain of the dying, and foretold futures to those who asked. For years, it was this way for her."

Claire paused for another sip of her drink, so I took the chance to ask her a question.

"Claire, where did she come from? Was she always living there?"

"No, Markus. No one ever knew where she came from. One day she was just there. It was like her house suddenly appeared on the beach, with her in it. Anyway, even back then people knew she had some sort of power, so they left her alone. Then, one by one, they would secretly visit her to get her help."

She took a bite of her now cold pizza and continued with the story.

"One day a man of great nobility came and beseeched her to help. His daughter had been attacked and killed by either a madman or a monster during the night one week prior. He explained that she was on her way home from the village and passed through the quiet woods that led to their manor home when it happened. She had been left for dead. A bite mark on her neck was all they found for a wound, but her body had been drained of its blood.

The nobleman asked her to tell what evil beast could do this. The witch searched through her old heavy books, flipping through the pages searching for the answer. She had done this many times before. She would turn to a page and would sense the correct villain. The noble stared in horror at the pictures of the monsters and unnamed things.

The witch was troubled because she could not get a feel for what did this awful thing. It was like something was missing. She asked the noble to tell her of the tragedy again, she needed more detail to pinpoint things better. He recounted the story. The same thing again, but the nobleman began to sob. Through his tears he asked the witch to also break the curse that had been placed on his daughter's body by the monster.

The witch asked him what the curse was. The man told her they had placed his daughter's body in the family crypt. It was a gracious resting place, 100 feet beneath the earth. There were barred windows in the ceiling to allow the sun to shine down upon the stone coffins. Only one way in, down a spiral stairs, three large locked stone doors kept thieves out.

They placed his daughter's lifeless body in a stone coffin and laid her to rest. That night the nobleman made his way to the crypt. He sat on a high hill where he could see the window to the crypt below. He told the witch he sat there in the moon light and cried over the death of his daughter. That was when the curse started. He heard the sound of grinding stone moving, and the screeching of his daughter's voice. Somehow she was alive. He did not know how, but she was in agony. He called down to her, but she would just curse at him and then start to scream again.

When the morning light came, the noble had his men open the tomb doors. But everything was as it should be. The coffins were in their right places. The heavy stone lids fixed atop them. The nobleman thought it must have been his grief playing tricks on him. So the next night he waited again for the sound of his daughter. Sure enough, when the moon was high, the sound of the grinding stone lid came again. He called to his daughter and once again she answered him with screams and anger. He stayed trying to calm her. The thought had crossed his mind to open the door of the crypt, but fear stopped him. He waited until daylight and again had his men open the three doors. Again, all was in the right place.

He decided the following day he would pay a large sum of money to the two traveling men who had stopped by his manor looking for work. He asked them to stay locked within the family crypt for the night. He told them there had been thieves and he wanted them to watch so he would know who it was. The two strangers agreed. They had been more than happy to take such easy work for such an large amount of money.

That night the nobleman once again took his place on the hill by the family grave. He eagerly watched and waited for the rising of the moon. Sure enough, as it came he heard the grinding stone. Instead of the retched screaming of his daughter, he heard her voice come soft and smooth, almost alluring, calling out. She seemed to have known that the two men were with her. They could not help themselves. They answered her. No sooner had they spoken to her, they screamed. The nobleman could hear the men yelling and crying for help, then came sounds of snapping – almost like bones being broken. There was silence, then his daughter's laughter pierced the night.

The nobleman wanted an answer so he found a young woman who could fix things. That is how he came to her cottage at the beach. He wanted to kill the monster who killed his daughter and put the retched curse on her that would not let her rest in her grave. He sat and waited for the witch to respond.

The young witch stood quiet. Finally, she walked to the window of her little home to gaze at the ocean. It turned dark and stormy. She looked back at the nobleman and told him she would return with him to his home to see first hand. She had heard stories of such creatures that would infect their prey. She opened another large volumed book that was hidden on a shelf and showed him. A picture of a plain man was drawn on the page. She explained they were lonely creatures that looked like men, and such they craved to be like men, to walk in the sun, to have companionship, to be alive.

The nobleman accepted the witch's offer. If she was right in her conclusion about the monster, he knew now what must be done to lay his daughter to rest. Why the witch choose to accompany him no one can say.

They arrived at the noble's manor the following day. He showed the witch the grave site and took her into the crypt. She looked around. The bodies of the two strangers were no where to be found. The witch suggested he pull the lid off his daughter's coffin, allowing the sunlight to fall on her body. She warned not to venture too close. If she had been cursed by the monster, the noble's daughter would surely kill who ever was in reach. Ropes were fastened to the lid of the coffin. The men stood far back and pulled with all their strength to expose the daughter's remains.

The bright sun shone directly on her lifeless body – nothing happen. A moment later that changed. Smoke rose from her body, then her eyes shot open and screams erupted from her mouth. She flew out of the coffin and tried to cower in the shadows, but it was pointless, because no shadows were big enough to protect her body, now blackened. The screams stopped and she fell to the floor shattering into millions of pieces.

The father cried. The witch explained this was not his daughter, but the curse animated and used her body. His daughter would now rest. As for the matter of the monster who infected her, well, the witch was sure he would feel what happened and run. She thought he did this to the girl to create himself a companion. Now she was gone and he would move on.

The noble thanked the witch and had his men escort her home.

The witch was right. The monster did move on. Not out of fear, but out of revenge. He followed her home.

There was a storm at sea as the witch looked through the windows of her cottage. Black clouds and flashes of lightning raged over the turbulent water. She sighed and closed her shutters. There was more than that one storm on the way.

Perhaps this was the way it was meant to be – or she had foreseen this happening – but the vampire followed her through the black night to her home. He watched her and waited. Perhaps for the perfect time to strike or maybe he was making the perfect plan to act out his revenge, we will never know."

Claire stopped the story. She yawned a little and grinned. She was clearly intoxicated; but so was I, so it really made no difference to me. A bathroom break was in order before she concluded her little story. I had to admit, I was finding it fascinating and was eager to hear more.

Once we were seated on the comfy couch with our glasses refilled, Claire returned to her story.

"What happened in the days or months the vampire watched the witch, there is nothing to tell – for some reason that part of the story was lost. But something did occur between the two. They now spent their time together. He knocked at her door at dusk and she would let him in. They would spend hours in conversation, seated across the room from each other. But as the time went on, they sat embraced in each other's arms.

Because she was a powerful witch, the vampire coveted her, or perhaps she could control his appetite by magical means, but the two seemed happy and content. Eventually they declared their love for each other – how the vampire could feel love is still unknown because they are heartless and souless. The pair sought a union – not a conventional marriage, but a ceremony deemed fitting for a witch. It was to be done in the hours of the morning sun. The vampire was willing to sacrifice himself to have this one moment with the witch, but it was not in her plans to lose him. So the night before the wedding, the witch gave her gift to her groom. The gift of tolerance to the light. An antidote to the sun. This spell was too powerful for the witch to conjure alone, so her mother had to complete it with her, though against her better judgement. She only did it out of her great love for her daughter.

From that moment on, the vampire and all those that were descended from his line would be safe from the rays of the light. The witch had hoped for a child. She did not know if she were to have one if it would be a witch or the undead. If her child were vampire, she wanted it protected with the spell.

The witch's mother secretly altered the spell. When the vampire walked during the unclouded day light hours, he would feel the effects of the sun like an irritating sunburn – minor, but irritating. His eyes would also water and sting if left unshielded.

The two were united. Happy they were, or so it seemed.

Time passed. But it was said that one day a tragedy occurred – the death of the young witch. The vampire was distraught, but the witch's mother knew he could not feel, so it must be a lie. She examined her daughter's body with care and found puncture wounds on her neck. The vampire had killed her. He tried to deny it saying it was in an attempt to bring her back to life after her passing. The mother saw through his rouse. She knew vampires were now sighted during the day throughout the countryside. She knew there was only one vampire who could pass on that allowance. She was certain he killed her daughter, now that he had what he wanted. He was building an army and she must stop him."

Claire shifted a little and sat quietly.

I waited for her to go on, but she didn't continue. I tried to get more out of her. "Come on Claire, what happened after that? Did the old mother get him and his army?"

She shook her head no and explained. "Nope. She went after him, but he got through her fingers. You know those bloodsuckers are slippery! And apparently they can steal magic too. So that's why he went after the young witch because she was so powerful. And now because of him, some of them can go in the daylight."

I looked at her. "What happened after that?"

"She searched for years, but never found him. All those that were created by him she destroyed. To this day the witchs descended from her make it their mission to seek revenge on those vampires who walk in the day in honour of the fallen young witch and the theft of her power and life."

We sat in silence for a few minutes as the story replayed in my mind. It was like a fairytale, yet there were things that rang true. It was something I would have liked to talked over with Darren. It left me with questions about him and vampires that I wanted answered.

Sensing what I was thinking, Claire interrupted my thoughts.

She stood up staggering away from the couch, turned and looked at me. "You know Markus, vampires would never admit to the truth of the story." She hiccupped and continued. "They're so selfish."

I smiled and slurred. "Well, when I finally meet one, I'll ask about it." I went to take a another sip of my glass but it was empty.

Claire giggled. "I am SO drunk! I really, really need to go home. Oooh that wine always gets to me."

I managed to stand up. "Okay, maybe we should call it a night." I tried to pick up the pizza box, but ended knocking it to the floor. "Oops, I guess I can get that in the morning."

We both laughed and slowly stumbled our way back down to the main floor of the store. We put on our coats and walked into cold. With a quick hug goodbye we parted ways. A large black cat followed after Claire. The walk home was blurry and cold. The whole time I smiled drunkenly and staggered. I had no concept of the time when I loudly and clumsily opened the front door of my building.

There was a loud bang and a flash of pink. Marge the land lady came out into the hall. "Whhaat are you doing?" She yelled in her thick Boston accent. "Do you know what time it is? I need my beauty sleep you know!"

Her face was furious, but I couldn't help but laugh. She wore a soft pink oversized robe, big pink rollers in her hair, and pink mud smeared all over her face.

I snorted. I was too drunk, and she looked so silly. "Sorry, I didn't mean to wake you."

I went upstairs, unable to contain myself at Marge's expense. I could hear her cursing at me, but it didn't matter. I didn't care at the moment.

I managed my keys in the door, threw my shoes off and went to my bedroom, collapsing on my bed. The room began to spin. I could feel my body start to heave. I pulled myself out of bed and ran to the bathroom, sick.

The cold of the floor felt soothing, as I lay my head on the tiles and closed my eyes. My head still spun, but it wasn't as bad, sleep was taking over now, and I was happy for it. Claire's story replayed in my mind, the vampire seducing the witch and stealing her power and finally killing her. Darren befriending me, becoming best friends, helping me with my secret and willingness, then I was nearly killed. Was it a plan to steal my power?

My mind shut down and I passed out.

CHAPTER EIGHT

THE HUNT

The next day was horrid.

A massive headache, queasy stomach and sensitive eyes were my only company. I was sore as I tidied up the bookshop. Claire wasn't in until late afternoon. I had the morning shift. So I was stuck with having to clean up our mess from the night before. "Oh well, I helped make it." I mumbled to myself.

Fortunately the day went by quickly. And Claire's shift finally started. We talked a little, worked and then as soon as my shift ended. I went home to sleep. I hoped Darren would be there. He wasn't.

Weeks passed and spring arrived. It was wet and dreary. There was still no sign of Darren. It was like he had never existed. Claire had developed a negative view of vampires lately and how their existence was only to be pests. She became an out and out vampire hater. Why she felt that way, I didn't know. It started the day Marge came to the bookshop looking for me for her rent money. Claire was stuck listening to her while I ran to a bank machine for cash.

As for me, I kept my opinion to myself. I was enthralled with vampires. But since meeting a few of them, I knew too well how very dangerous they were. I had never mentioned it to Claire, but somehow she knew.

She still forced me to help her practice her spells. Some of the tricks were really good and some she needed to work on. She continued to make references to me such as "Markus just *will* it to happen and ask for a sign." It was odd, there was no way she could have known my secret.

I felt like I was caught in the middle of something I had no place in. Claire raised some good points of vampires stealing the powers of witches. It helped them become stronger, protect themselves against others, live longer and better, even though they were immortal. Also she said it aided them in some unnameable practices of dark magic. It was her favourite subject, I think. Some of it did make sense – I knew Darren would never be like that – but as time went on, I grew less and less sure.

Claire said on occasion the vampires would share the magic with others. Sometimes as an offering to make amends or peace with each other. "Vampires are all evil and hate each other and even themselves." She said. "So the peace thing was some devious plot to take out the other guy."

I thought, "Maybe Darren was using me for some reason, maybe as a gift to make up to his sister Chloe." I knew this was untrue. He would never have done this, but he wasn't around to ask, and Claire reminded me of that every day.

It was a little unfair to me – this whole situation. Claire was a good friend, and she had a way of making me smile with just her pure silliness and simple disposition. But now, I was starting to feel like I was detaching from her. She was becoming incredibly negative. It forced me to keep thinking of Darren and wishing he was back.

Claire was bullying me to help her with her magic now. She was trying more advanced spells or so she said. I got the feeling they went against all of the old Claire's rules. The new Claire didn't care, and was mean, putting Darren down and yelling at me.

I wasn't enjoying my time with her anymore. But there was no way around it. All of my shifts were with her. I couldn't quit because I needed the money. The more time I was with her, the more drained I felt.

I needed something to change. Why couldn't it be back the way it used to be?

I walked down the back street towards work. I needed a sign that I could escape from this for a little while. Maybe it was all in my mind. Maybe it was just me feeling sorry for myself, missing Darren and taking it out on Claire. Maybe she was still the same great friend and I was the one who had changed?

I continued to walk, the sun gently lowering. "Darren, where are you? I need you."

I stopped and put my head in my hands. There was no one around, and it was a good thing. It seemed like I finally hit a breaking point. I started to sob. Everything that had happened to me came crashing at once. Memories and fears from my attacks, the loss of Darren and the issues with Claire came from every side. I was frozen. Tired and broken.

I sunk to my knees. The pavement was wet and cold. It went through my jeans. I really didn't care. There wasn't too much I cared about at this moment. My head was spinning and I was about to be sick. I couldn't get a hold of one thought long enough to break out of this. I felt a strong vibration go through my body and an all too familiar surge. Then everything went black.

What was seconds could have been hours, or days, for all I knew. I finally opened my eyes. It was dim. I could feel warmth around me. My hands felt the soft blanket that was spread over me. I had no idea where I was.

I sprang up in a state of panic. My head spun. My knees buckled.

Then strong hands caught me. They slowly helped me down and gently pulled the blanket back over me.

A soft light turned on somewhere in the room.

Darren stared at me as he quietly kneeled beside me. I reached out my hand and touched his face. Was it really him? Was he here?

"Dare?" My hand felt the short prickly hair on his head. "Is it you?"

He looked at the ground. "Yes Markus, please rest."

I sat up quickly and embraced him in a tight hug. He tensed, but I could feel his resistance slide.

I let go. "Darren ..." Tears started to come. I didn't know why I was being so emotional. "Please Darren, don't go. Please!"

He put his cold hand on my arm. "Markus, I'm not going anywhere."

I wiped the wet away from my eyes, but it wouldn't stop. "Why did you leave? Where were you? How could you do that?" The flood gates of questions were starting to come.

Darren sat quiet, then he held his hand, "Markus, first know this – I never meant to hurt or worry you, I only sought to protect you." He lifted himself off the floor and sat on the couch. "I felt that you were safe here on your own. You were starting to be yourself again. You had Claire, so I thought it a good time to look for Alex. I wanted to find him and make sure that he never looked for you again. I left that night without telling you to avoid you stopping me. Besides, you were a little tired of my presence and you could use the space."

Darren looked to the floor and paused. It was then that I noticed we were sitting in his bedroom.

He continued. "I never found Alex. I searched every place I could think of. I returned to England and looked there for him and my sister. I don't know whether Chloe has a part in this. Most times she cannot be bothered to do anything at all – she lives to be waited upon. But I wanted to be sure, just in case. I returned home when I heard and felt you call to me. I couldn't resist and I came to you as fast as I could. I found you alone in an alley crumpled on the ground. No one would have seen you until the morning. I was so worried. I just wanted you safe again."

He stood up and began pacing.

I pulled the blanket off, got up and walked to where he was. He looked at me and stood still. Darren began to speak, but I reached up and put my finger on his lips. I had something I wanted to say.

"Darren, please, you don't have to worry about me. I would rather have you here to keep me company and go through everything all over again than have you gone. You're really important to me. You're the only best friend I've ever had, and the only one who knows everything about me."

He reached his hand slowly up and rested it on the back of my neck. He looked into my eyes for a moment, as if searching for something. He swallowed hard and pulled me to him.

Like a quick change of heart, Darren wrapped his arms around and caught me in a tight hug. It felt like he was going to break my ribs if he didn't loosen his grip. I hugged him back, although I didn't have the same strength as him. He didn't seem to mind.

We stepped apart. Darren was happy now. His face had softened. He walked towards the door and motioned for me to follow him.

We went down to the kitchen and he fixed me something to eat. I gobbled it up in no time at all. Darren made some coffee and then sat down beside me.

"So?" He said. "What were you up to while I was gone? Did you get into any trouble?"

I took a swig of the hot coffee. "Well, no, I just worked a lot. But Claire got really weird. All of the sudden she became a vampire hater or something!"

Darren's lips tightened and his jaw clenched.

I continued quickly. "No, she doesn't know about you. It's not like she goes hunting for vampires. She told me this story about some witch on a beach who married a vampire and he killed her after she made him a spell to be able to go into the sun or something. So I guess some witches hate vampires because of it."

I took another sip of the coffee. "Dare, is that true? Are there vampires that can go in the sun and some that can't? Sorry, I don't mean to pry or anything. I'm just curious. Because I know you have been in the sun, so I wasn't sure if it was true, the story and all that."

I sat quiet for a moment and watched Darren's face relax a little.

"Yes, Markus, it is true. There are those of us who can tolerate the sun, and those that would burn away in it. It has been that way for many, many years. There is a certain animosity between the two of our kinds. Once you are made a vampire of the night, there is no way to be tolerant of the sun."

I raised an eye brow. "So, like if you made me a vampire, I would still be able to go in the sunlight, right?"

He smirked. "Yes, *theoretically*, if I made you a vampire, you would have the abilities of my kind."

"So the whole story of the witch getting married and killed is true?"

"NO. Most certainly not. Our kind has existed for thousands of years. There might have been some witch who made a spell to help a night vampire, but that is not how our tolerance started. It sounds like some old witch family has a score to settle – or had a bad run in – and is trying to place blame."

"Oh, I guess that would explain it." I shifted in my chair. "I should let Claire know. That way she won't be so worked up about vampires She told me that vampires could steal powers from witches, and she said some pretty weird things, like she kind of hinted that maybe you were trying to steal my abilities or something."

"WHAT? You didn't tell her about your gift did you? I thought you said she didn't know about me either? Markus, did you say anything at all?"

"No, of course I didn't. It was strange, like I said, it's like she just knew things. But that is when she was getting all weird. I didn't want to be around her anymore. Everyday she tried to drill into my head that vampires were evil and needed to be killed, or they would steal from all the witches to conquer the world."

"Markus, I think you need to stay away from Claire for the moment. That opinion doesn't sound like the real her. Her and her fairies believe in a very peaceful existence. They believe we might not all like each other, but we must respect the other and coexist."

Darren got up and refilled my coffee. I was a little shocked at Darren's response. He believed in Claire's fairies?

"Dare?"

"Yes?"

"Uhmm, are you saying the fairies are real?"

"Yes, they are. I'm not saying all types of fairies that people write about are real, but the ones Claire speaks with are very real."

"Oh. I just assumed ... she was on some cheap drugs some days!"

"*Markus*, come on. I exist, so why can't there be other things?"

I sat silent for a moment. It was a little much for me to take in

– that part of the fictional world was actually real. Since moving to Boston my eyes were opening up. What other things were real? I tried to think of other books I read at the bookstore ...

"Oh no! Dare, I need to call work. I'm supposed to be working with Claire."

Darren got up and brought the phone over. "Markus, tell them you are really sick and couldn't make it in. Got it? I don't want you going back there right now. You need rest and you need to stay away from Claire."

"Okay, got it." I agreed with Darren. Something with Claire wasn't right.

She answered the phone at the store. I faked a sick voice and repeated what Darren had told me. But before I hung up, she told me I needed to come in as a package had arrived for me. It was from a Ms. Havish. What could she have sent me? Memories flooded my mind. She was the only person who had been like a parent or a guardian during my youth. I needed to see what it was.

I covered the mouthpiece of the phone, and asked Darren what to do. It was really important to me. He had heard everything as his hearing was better than any humans. He said to tell Claire he would pick it up for me before the store closed.

When I told her, she was silent for a minute, than finally said "Fine." She hung up.

"Dare, thank you!"

I explained to him about Ms. Havish being my sanctuary from childhood bullying. He understood.

I finished my coffee as Darren got up.

"Well, Markus, I'll leave now and go get that for you. Please stay in the house and don't wander off. There's lots of food, beer, etc."

He opened a cupboard and threw a bag of barbeque chips on the counter top.

"My fav. Thanks Dare."

We walked to the front door of the house. Darren opened it then turned to me. "Please Markus, just stay put. It's too dark to be outside when you don't know your way around."

"I know. You worry too much Dare."

He smiled as he walked out into the front driveway. The large lamp of the overhang lit a wide area, including Darren's car. The SUV was not in sight. He got in his car and started it, pulling away slowly, waving as he did so. He drove out of sight.

A cold breeze blew past me. There was a crackling of branches. A sudden nervousness overcame me. It was like something was standing in the dark of the trees. Something on the opposite end of the driveway. I felt afraid and in danger. I quickly closed the front door and locked it. I ran back to Darren's room.

The last of the setting sun had disappeared. The woods that surrounded the house were in darkness. All was silent and still. I could feel something was out there, watching, waiting. The hairs on my arms stood on end. Darren had chosen a bad time to leave me alone.

I stood in the glass room at the top of his house. It was safe here, at least I could see most of the property. I looked out as far as possible. Straining my eyes, I looked this way and that, still nothing. But I couldn't shake the fear. Maybe it was knowing I was in the middle of nowhere alone, maybe not. Nothing could get into the house, unless there was a window or door open. "What if there is?" I yelled in panic.

I ran down the stairs from the glass room into Darren's room and into the hall. My heart was racing as I went into the living room.

The curtains were pushed open. The dark trees outside stood still. I made sure the glass French doors were all locked. My throat ached with terror. I didn't want to be anywhere near those doors. The fact that I knew something out there could crash through at me at any time raced through my brain.

I pulled the heavy curtains closed, shutting out the view of the trees. The room around me was now darker, cold, I started to back out of it slowly, reaching behind me for the door. I found it and jumped into the hallway, slamming the door closed.

I stood and caught my breath for a moment. Where did I need to check next? The main bathroom had no windows. Darren's room didn't have windows that opened, at least I didn't think they could.

"The kitchen!"

I bounded down the main steps two at a time. I went through the kitchen door and hurried over to the sliders. They were both locked. There were no curtains here to pull closed. As a last minute thought, I went to the fridge and grabbed a few drinks and the bag of chips off the counter, just in case I got hungry and didn't have the nerve to come down later.

As I walked through the front hall the smell of the trees filled my nose. It was oddly calming, mixed with the faint cool breeze that swept around me. I froze. The front door was open.

I put everything down on the hall table. Slowly, I walked to the big heavy wooden door. "Darren?" I called. "Hello?"

There was no reply.

Instead of slamming the door closed, and locking myself in Darren's room, my curiosity got the better of me.

I stepped outside into the front entrance. The overhead light shone down and the entire area was visible. Again I called out. "Darren, is that you? Hello? Is anyone there?"

Nothing.

Slowly, I walked to the furthest edge of the light. Nothing but trees and blackness was there. Yet, I thought I could make out something in the distance, like a shape. I squinted and leaned forward to try to make out what I was seeing. My eyes adjusted to the darkness.

It looked like a small patch of white. No, it wasn't as small as I thought, my eyes refocused and the white expanded. There was definitely something there. I blinked and it disappeared. Maybe I was wrong.

"Hello?" I whispered.

I stepped back towards the safety of the house and backed fully in the light of the lamp above. My heart pounded in my chest. A branch snapped. The silence was broken and I jumped.

Another branch snapped. I could see white again. This time it was moving towards me. I continued my backwards retreat into the house, keeping my sights fixed on the unknown thing that was slowly making its way.

Suddenly, I hit something hard. The door. I needed to get inside, but I froze. The white unknown was close and taking shape. It was at the edge of the lit overhang. Still shrouded in darkness. Maybe it feared the light. I was holding my breath, waiting to see what would happen. All logical thinking had escaped me. I stood in fright.

First, a shoed foot appeared followed by jean-clad legs. Then a torso in a white hooded sweater, then a head. A white baseball cap covered the face.

I swallowed. "Hello? Can I help you?"

Laughter, then a response. "Oh, that you can buddy."

Waves of terror washed over me. "Oh my god ...No, no, please, leave me alone, please!" I shook violently. Alex had found me.

He looked up at me. His face now visible in the light, dark sunglasses still covered his eyes. An evil smile crept across his face. "Oh, come on buddy. I know you missed me. If you didn't want me to find you, you would have hid a little better."

"Please, just leave me alone ..." I pushed myself back through the front door of the house. "I don't want to die." I was crying. "Just leave me alone ..."

I started to sob and tremble. Alex grinned ear to ear. His sharp white teeth were clearly visible. He stepped closer to me but stopped a few feet away.

"Tell you what buddy. I will give you a two minute head start to run and hide. How's that sound? Not going to do you much good, because I *will* find you! Then you are going to suffer, and that boyfriend of yours is going to suffer. Then everyone will be happy."

"WHY ARE YOU DOING THIS TO ME?" I screamed, despair made me lose control.

"Because buddy, it's a favour, and besides, I'm having fun." He snickered. "Your two minutes starts now."

Alex jumped forward and pushed me into the house, he pulled the front door closed, with me on the inside and him on the outside. I heard him start to count loudly.

Panicking, I stood for a moment not sure of what was actually happening. Then my adrenaline kicked in. I leapt up the stairs as fast as I could, running into Darren's room. I closed the door and locked it then dragged a nearby chair and pushed it against the door. I went into Darren's bathroom locking the door. There was no where else to go, or hide. It was impossible to run faster than Alex.

He would have me in a flash out in the woods. I had to stay here and barricade myself and hope that Darren would make it back in time to save me.

A light bulb clicked on in my brain. "Darren, help! Alex is here, I *need* you to be here now. I *will* it. Darren be here ..."

I heard Alex's voice in the house. "Ready or not, here I come."

I slid to the bathroom floor. What could I to do?

Then was a knock at the door. "Markus? Are you in there? Come on buddy, you could have found a better hiding spot then that." He started to laugh.

The door was ripped off its hinges and thrown backwards. Alex stood in the room with a cruel smirk on his face. He came towards me. I had nowhere to go now. He stood by my feet. Then he squatted down and spoke.

"Oh come on buddy, don't look so sad. I ain't going to kill you."

I stared at him, my heart skipped a beat. Did I hear wrong? Was he going to let me go?

"What? But I thought ... you wanted to kill me ..." My voice trailed off.

Alex stood up. "Buddy I *do*! But, all I am going to do is hurt you." He smirked. "Real Bad." He started to laugh uncontrollably. Clearly enjoying himself at the expense of my terrified look.

Effortlessly, he picked me up with one hand and carried me up the stairs from Darren's room to the glass room.

He threw me down on the couch. "You see buddy, I'm going to have my fun with you. Take out all my frustrations, and leave you with only a thread of life in your body. That way, when your boyfriend comes home, he will be heart broken, and you know how he feels about you. He will have to choose whether to turn you or let you die.

He will let you die you know. After what happened the last time he made a mate and what that mate ended up doing, he will never let it happen again. But eventually it will tear him apart, choosing to let you go. He will spend an eternity hating himself and regretting his decision. And, my darling Chloe will be happy and finally have her revenge. So, why don't we begin?"

Alex bent down over me, inhaling over my torso then up to my neck. My body tensed. He lifted his face for me to see – it looked evil and crazed, his white fangs protruded.

He lunged at my throat. The pain was agonizing and it burned as he tore his teeth in. My body was trying to recoil, but he was too powerful, too strong. He stopped for a brief moment to speak. Blood running down his chin.

"Oh, you have quite the interesting taste, very foreign, no wonder he wanted you around. No matter. It's too late for him now."

Alex pulled my weakened body off the couch and thrust me into the window. The glass was thick and I bounced off it. He grabbed me from the floor and slammed me against another window. Again and again and again he did this. I couldn't breath, the pain was too much. Yet so afraid, I couldn't make a sound. I couldn't even cry.

He scratched and scraped at my torso, cutting me open with his nails. He chewed into my arm and drank. He flung me to the ceiling and kept a firm grip on my arm. I felt the sheer hell of it dislocating and the bones shatter. I screamed. He looked at my face and grinned. Again he attacked and ripped into my neck. I wanted to die. I couldn't take anymore. My entire body wreathed in pain.

Alex dropped me to the floor. His face and glasses were blood smeared, and his clothes were also splattered with the deep wet crimson. He grinned and spoke.

"You don't look so good buddy. I hope it was as good for you as it was for me?" He chuckled. "What's the matter, hurt too much to talk? If you hadn't noticed, I left your ears and eyes alone. That way you can watch and hear Darren's horror of finding you like this. Should be a real scream. But now I will leave you to die, I have to go find that fat magician friend of yours and thank her for letting me know where to find you. Then I can get rid of her. Been nice knowing you, buddy."

With that, Alex kicked my body as hard as he could – my ribs shattered. It hurt too much to react. I couldn't move or make a sound as he left. All I was capable of doing was crying. The tears poured down my face. I wished to die. It was all I could think of and all that I wanted.

Minutes passed, then somewhere, I heard a yell. The glass shattered all around me. I closed my eyes to avoid the shards. I felt the pain of being lifted. It felt I was being crushed.

I opened my eyes.

Darren was cradling me in his arms with all his strength like a child who refuses to let go of their favourite teddy bear ... Pinkish tears ran down his cheeks as he rocked me gently. He looked at my face, then noticed there was still life in my body.

"Markus? Markus? I'm sorry. I tried to get here. I'm so sorry!" He dropped his head down and held my broken body tighter.

He looked at me again. I could see the twisted agony on his face. Alex was right. Darren was torn, he was contemplating a decision in his mind and it was tearing him apart.

He spoke again, sobbing. "Markus? Please forgive me. I don't know why they did this. I never wanted anyone to hurt you. I am so sorry. Please forgive me. Please!"

Darren lay me down on the couch and knelt down beside me. He looked over my bloody mangled body. I could see from the reaction on his face, there was no hope for me.

He wiped at his eyes to clear the tears away. He took a deep breath, staring me in the eyes.

"Markus, There is something I want you to know. I need you to hear it." He grabbed my hand and gently held it. He wiped more pink tears away from his eyes. "Markus ... I ... I ... love you ... I never wanted you to be hurt. I want to save you ... but ... I can't! I mustn't! You are not meant to be cursed. But you deserve better than to die this way."

Darren lay his head on my chest and wept loudly. The pain in my body was disappearing, I felt light and almost calm. The lights and images brightened. Peace was overtaking me.

Darren jolted up. He looked at me. His eyes darted back and forth in a panic. He mumbled something to himself. His expression was unsure and crazed.

The lights were steadily growing brighter all around me. The pain was almost completely gone now. It was like I was starting to float off the couch. I wanted more of it. Darren's eyes bore into mine. So sad he was, I wanted to comfort him. I wanted to rid him of his pain. I would miss him.

I wanted to tell him I would have stayed here with him. I needed to thank him, but I couldn't. The light was getting brighter, and now I was trying to back away from it. It was too soon, I wasn't ready yet. I need a little more time, just a few moments more ...

The pain shot back into my body. I focused my eyes. Darren was there, with blood dripping from his mouth. I didn't understand what was happening.

I felt cold drops in my mouth. Then it started to pour down my throat. An ice cold river was now flowing into my entire body. It started to freeze, to burn. I contorted and flexed. I could feel all of my broke bones, rips and tears. Twisting, I tried to get away from the pain. The freezing still stung inside and the hot burn of my injuries pulsed on the outside. I squirmed and fell to the floor in torment. Rolling, I lashed my limbs outwards in all directions. I needed it to stop. My body did not respond. It was pure pain and agony. I felt my body lift itself and smack into the glass window. More burning. I was rolled on the floor again.

"DARREN! HELP!! Please ..."

My body lurched up into the air then fell hard to the floor. I shuddered. My heart beat skipped.

Darren's hand was on my face, a cold comfort. "Markus, I will make it stop. I will make all the pain go away. It won't hurt you anymore."

"Help me please Dare..." I whispered.

"I will Markus. Forgive me."

An intense flash of pure agony. I screamed. My chest heaved and clenched. I was numb. The air in my lungs escaped me, my heart pounded then stopped.

Blackness.

CHAPTER NINE
THE RISING

I opened my eyes and took a sharp inhale of air. It was like I had been holding my breath under water. I sat up quickly, my body ached and a dull throbbing was in my head. Was I dead? Was this a dream? What happened?

My eyes focused on the soft light in the corner of the room. Darren stood with his back towards me looking out his bedroom window. I adjusted and sat myself up. My head pounded harder. It felt like a bad hangover, mixed with dééjàà vu. Darren noticed I was awake and walked towards me.

"How do you feel, Markus?" He asked.

"Uhmm, a little sore. Man, did I hit my head or drink too much? What a head ache!"

Darren laughed softly. "Well, yes, you did get tossed around a bit. But you're okay now. Soon enough the aching will go away."

Shaking my head, I tried to separate my memories from the nightmare I had. I looked up at Darren, his flawless face seemed to glow a little, his eyes had a soft iridescence about them. Funny, I had never noticed it before. My stomached growled. I held my hand to it. The skin of my abdomen was sore to the touch.

"Oh geez, my whole body hurts." My mind was hazy. "I can't even remember what happened, Dare. It was like a nightmare. What an awful dream. Alex showed up here. He chased me. He was going to kill me. Wait, actually, in the dream he said he was going to hurt me really bad or something, so I was almost dead, then you would let me die or turn me into a vamp. But since what happened last time to the guy you made – you know the one who killed your sister's husband – Alex said you would let me die, then you would go crazy and tear yourself apart, then Chole would be happy and have her revenge. Then he attacked me, bit my neck, threw me around. Then he was going to go after Claire cause she told him I was here, but he was going to kill her next! It was awful."

Darrens face was full of rage. An anger like I had never seen.

"WHAT? Chloe was behind this? Is that what he said Markus? She would think I would ever let you die!"

Darren got up and walked quickly over to the opposite end of the room and looked out into the dark trees. His arms at his side, fist clenched.

A sinking feeling was in my stomach. Standing up slowly, I became aware of the pain in my legs. I looked down at my bare skin. Faint scratches and bruises covered me. My body looked pale. I swallowed hard.

"Dare ... What happened? Dare ... Oh my god ... DARREN, what happened to me?"

I began to trembled.

Darren was at my side in a flash. He caught my arm and walked me over to his closet. He opened the door. Inside the little room was a bench and a full length mirror. He walked me to it. I was speechless as I gazed at my near naked reflection. My entire body was covered in patches of white, pink, brown, grey and purple. I could see the outlines of where my flesh had been torn and ripped, but it was healing. My blue eyes sparkled, the whites around them shone, as did the white of my teeth.

Darren turned to me, his face serious. He opened his mouth

to speak.

"Markus. That was no dream. It was real. And yes, I was faced with a decision to let you die, or to make you one of my kind." He let his head sink down and looked at the floor. He took a deep inhale then started. "So I chose Markus. I chose not to lose you. I thought it was something that you would have wanted if the decision was yours to make. If I'm wrong, then forgive me."

Silence.

Finally, I turned to him. I held up my arm and looked at it. It looked dead. Was it possible? Was I now something that I had always dreamed about? Was I now like Darren? Immortal?

"Darren? Am I a vampire?" I swung round to look at him. I wanted it to be true, but it still scared me.

"Yes Markus, you are."

"Really? You're not joking are you? I'm a vampire, like you?" I smiled widely.

Darren looked shocked. "You're okay with this Markus? I mean you're not angry with me for doing this to you?"

Was Darren serious? Many emotions went through my head, but anger wasn't one of them. I had fantasized about worlds with vampires for so long. I can't believe I was now part of it. I didn't know what to say.

"No. Not at all." I marvelled at myself in the mirror. " I always dreamt about it. It kind of sucks that I had to be beaten to a pulp to have this happen. Thank you for saving me."

My skin was different – it was muted, the feel of it, even the smell of it. My head started to swim. Has this really happened? There were so many things I wanted to know. Where do I start? I gazed in the mirror again, I didn't look perfect like Darren or his sister.

"Dare, am I gonna look all weird and multi-coloured forever?"

"No, it will go away in a few days. You were in such a bad state your body has to heal now. Besides, you're new, so it takes it a little longer. When you are my age you will heal pretty quickly."

"Oh, okay I get it. I guess there are a lot of things that you'll need to tell me about. So how did you turn me? Did you just bite me or something?"

"There is a little more to it than that. I had to drain you until your heart stopped beating. Then I gave you my blood which started the transformation ..."

We stood there for a moment. I got distracted by my hands, they felt like my hands, but looked foreign. I turned them over studying both sides. Vampire hands ... my hands. All because of Alex. I still couldn't believe what had happened.

"You know Dare, I'm glad Alex did it. Tried to kill me, I mean. I'm actually a vampire now." A grin spread across my face.

"It's sadistic to be thankful for that type of pain Markus. But I understand. It's not the way I would have chosen to turn you. Eventually, one day, I would have done it for you if you had asked. I would have hated doing it, but I would have done it."

"Oh." I hesitated. "I thought you wanted me to hang around? It didn't occur to me that you felt forced into it. I'm sorry, Darren." How stupid could I be? I had honesty believed Darren had wanted me to stay with him. Now he was stuck with me.

"No. Markus. Of course I want you to stay here. I only meant that I would have hated to inflict any pain on you. Don't be stupid."

"I get it now. Sorry Dare. So ... Uhmm, what next?" Excitement to start living my new life was building.

Darren turned and picked up a pile of clothes off the bench, and tossed them at me.

"Here, why don't you put these on for starters. Vampires don't usually walk around in their underwear." He smirked and looked me up and down.

"Good idea." I put my jeans on, then a thought occurred to me. "Dare, uhmm, does it work? I mean, you know ... My uhmm ..." I looked down at myself.

Darren smiled. "Yes, Markus, you can still have sex. It feels somewhat different, but it's still good."

"Well, I guess I won't know the difference since I don't have anything to compare."

Darren's eyes widened in shocked. "What? You're a virgin? You're kidding me?"

"No, no one ever bothered with me. Besides, I'm nothing to look at."

He raised his eyebrow. "Nothing to look at? Markus, you are quite beautiful, so just stop it."

"Gee thanks Darren. I'm glad someone thinks so!"

He blushed.

I finished changing and we walked out of the closet into Darren's room. We walked towards the staircase that lead up to the glass room. I was a little afraid to go up, but I wanted to see just how bad it was. Taking the steps two at a time, I sped up them faster than humanly possible. It must be my new vampire skills. Man was I fast.

I felt the moist breeze that came in from the hole in the glass wall. Shards of glass were everywhere. The furniture was broken. Blood covered it all. It was splattered, smeared and hand printed across the walls. There were dried pools covering the floor. I couldn't believe how much there was. It shocked me. But I couldn't fully grasp how bad it was. Because I was too distracted. The sweet smell in the room caught my nose. I breathed in deeply. It made me hungry. My body craved it. I realized it was the blood. I was a vampire now, and the blood called to me.

I stepped back. What was I supposed to do? My teeth started to ache. My mouth was dry. I glanced quickly around the room, all of the blood had dried up. Turning around, I went back down the stairs. Darren stood and waited for me.

"Markus, just breathe deeply. It will pass. You will have to learn to control it."

"I CAN'T! I'm so hungry. It hurts, Darren, it hurts." I cupped my mouth as if trying to make the ache go away.

He came closer to me. "Can't you fight it? I would give you mine, but it would change things."

"I don't care. Please I need it." The aching worsened. "Please Dare."

"Markus, We would be connected together forever." He shook his head. "You need to be free to make your own choice. Not tied to me for an eternity."

I grabbed his shoulders. Pain was building in my head. It felt like it was about to explode. "Darren, I want to stay with you! Haven't you figured it out yet?"

I fell to my knees. I had no strength left. I was in agony.

Darren swept down and lifted me up. He carried me to the couch and lay me down. He placed his wrist to my mouth. "Take it." Was all that he said.

I closed my eyes and bit. My new teeth effortlessly pierced his skin, like cutting into warm butter. Cold blood filled my mouth. It had a burn to it despite its chill. The taste was better than anything

I had ever experienced. An overwhelming euphoric feeling swept over me. It was intense. It was like floating, spinning, drifting gently on the breeze. The cold burn filled my veins.

My skin started to tingle as I opened my eyes. There was Darren looking down. I felt connected to him. It was as if our entire bodies were touching yet there was distance between us. I wanted to take him and wrap him around my body like a blanket, just so the feeling would last.

Darren pulled his wrist away. I wanted more, but I knew somehow he had reached his limit. He needed me to stop and be happy with what he offered. I was. I sat up. It was if I had slept for days and feasted like a king. I felt on top of the world. Darren was gladdened with my contentment. There was a relaxation in him, he let his guard down. Funny how I read Darren so well. I was never great with reading people. He was amused with my thought.

"Darren?"

"Yes, Markus?"

"Uhmm, something weird is happening!"

He smiled. "What do you think is weird?"

I felt his humour, his playfulness surrounded me. "It's like I know what you're thinking. It's bizarre."

"Actually, Markus. You're sensing my emotions. I can feel yours too. Remember I mentioned about us sharing blood, there would be a connection? Well, this is what I was talking about. This is the bond we will share for the rest of eternity – we'll be able to feel each others sadness, happiness, amusement – all sorts of feelings I am guessing. Vampires who decide to connect share different bonds. But it's random what that connection will be and this is what we got."

My eyes opened wide. "Whoa ... This is so cool. So, like what if

I'm on the other side of the world or something? Do you think we can feel each other?"

"I have no idea how it will work with distance. But if you ever plan a last minute vacation without me, I bet we will have the answer." Darren smirked. "I'm relieved you can't read my thoughts. That might have been a little uncomfortable or even embarrassing."

His humour swirled around me. What a odd sensation it was. It was like physically feeling emotions. It was as if I could hold them or pull them around me. I raised my arms up to try, noticing my skin had returned to its original colour. I looked normal again, no scars, no multi-coloured flesh. I lifted my shirt to look at my stomach to see if I was healed all over.

My skin had indeed healed. Actually it was even better than before. My stomach muscles were harder and sharper. My body was more defined and toned. I was somehow in better shape.

An aroused sensation floated around me. I looked up at Darren. His face blushed and he quickly turned away. I guess he felt my appreciation of my new body.

"Sorry, Dare. That was my fault. Just it's amazing how different I feel, my body is fit and in wicked shape now. I can be proud of it for once in my life. This is all so cool. I wish I could show Claire."

Dread overcame me.

"Oh my god, Claire. I forgot about her. Alex is going to kill her. Darren we have to go help her."

I paced back and forth unsure of what to do. Also afraid of seeing Alex again. Who knew what he would try to do to me if he seen me now.

Darren spoke. "Okay, let's go. But I'm sure Claire will be fine Markus. Her little friends will look out for her. Believe me, I have seen what they are capable of."

I knew he was telling the truth and he felt confident in what he said. I accepted that fact, but I still worried.

We raced to Darren's car and got in. He started it and we sped away. With my new vision skills, I could see everything clearly. I could make out the details of the things we drove past. I was enthralled with it all. The bark of the trees, so intricate. The way the wetness clung to the bare branches. The life that crawled on the forest floor, waking for the spring. I felt like a child in a toy store. My eyes wide, trying to take it all in.

Finally, we arrived. I had been too preoccupied to worry about Claire, and felt guilty for it now. But Darren still believed strongly that she would be alright. He pulled over to the side of the road opposite the bookstore. The closed sign was in the window, but the lights were still on. I looked at the clock on the dashboard. It was 9:36pm. Claire should still be there, the store only closed at 9:30.

I reached for the door handle, Darren stopped me. "No. Markus, wait a minute. We really need to be careful in there."

"I know. I know. I just want to make sure Claire is okay."

"Markus, I mean *you* need to be careful. Alex might be in there. If he sees you now, he will try to kill you."

He was uneasy, but I already figured that would probably happen anyway.

"Dare it's fine. I'm sure I can take him now. Besides, I've got you to help me, right?"

I smiled dumbly. I couldn't help it. Darren wouldn't let anything happen to me. He would crush Alex if he tried.

"Markus, you haven't had a chance to use your body the way it is now. You'll be a little clumsy and overextend yourself. Just please be careful and if I tell you to get out of the way, please do it."

"Alright. I will. Thanks for the pep talk *dad*, can we go save Claire now?"

Darren rolled his eyes.

We got out and crossed the street. I pulled at the front door. To my surprise it was unlocked. Claire always remembered to lock the door. It was the first thing she would do when we closed the store. Something wasn't right.

We went in and I locked the door behind me. I didn't need some innocent person getting hurt by Alex. Inside, everything was were it should be. The smell of the coffee filled my nose, it was putrid. How did I ever drink that?

Darren chuckled quietly and whispered. "Why do you think I always brought you a coffee? The stuff you drank here was swill."

No one was around on the main floor. Something glittery on the floor by the front counter caught my attention. I walked over to it and squatted down. It was one of Claires butterfly hair clips. She would have noticed if she lost it, I was sure.

I showed Darren. "She must still be here. I hope she's okay."

It was odd how quiet it was as we climbed the stairs to the second floor of the store. We stepped lightly to avoid making any noise, but I was sure, who ever was here knew that we were here.

We reached the landing. Directly in front of us were the couches where Claire had told me the story of the beach witch and vampire. To my surprise, there sat Claire, looking at ease. She was engrossed in small blue book. Next to her with knees bent and legs crossed, looking picture perfect and demure – was Chloe. Her long, straight black hair was fanned out across her bare shoulders. With her pale flawless skin, she could have been mistaken for a statue.

Chloe didn't blink or react when she saw me. She held up her hand and called to Darren in her sweetest French accent.

"My dear brother. What a surprise. What brings you to me?" She smiled sweetly, batting her eyes, looking innocent.

"I was not expecting to see you sister. But how fortunate for me." Darren smiled, but it was a cruel smile, one that spoke volumes.

Chloe gently stood up. It was as if she was a queen, raising herself for her subjects. She stepped toward Darren, then stopped and stared at me.

"You!" She pointed her finger at me. "You should be dead. I see I underestimated what you mean to my brother. No matter, I will take care of you later."

Darren stepped in front of me. "I would not try it if I were you, Chloe. Go back home, leave us be. You have done enough damage."

Alex appeared out of the shadows and walked to her side. He sported his sunglasses as usual. Chloe acknowledge him. "What took you so long cher? Leaving me waiting in this pit of a place."

Alex took her hand and kissed it. "Sorry my love, I needed to clean up. I had stains from some filthy human." He faced me.

"Buddy, look at you. Not even a scratch left. That's a shame. Maybe I should have torn you to bits and scattered the pieces all over." He laughed loudly. "I always like leaving some sort of mark, maybe I can rip an ear off or something else right now."

Alex lunged forward. Before I could blink Darren had him pinned to the floor. He spat and pushed with all his strength to force Darren off. Again he flew at me. I tried to side step him, but he caught me, knocking me to the ground. His sharp white fangs protruded from his mouth. I grabbed hold of his neck and squeezed. We rolled across the floor.

Suddenly, Alex was yanked off of me by Darren, who harshly flung him across the room. Alex got up and charged. Darren slammed his body into Alex. The sound of crushing bones echoed in the store. Alex lay sprawled out. This time he was slower to get up. He snarled and looked from Darren to me as if deciding who was the easier prey. He came at me. I hurled myself at him. We collided, locking arms and started to struggle. My own fangs protruded, aching to rip at him. We bounced off shelves and sent books flying. We backed into the couch and tumbled to the floor.

We were broken apart. I was set aside. Alex was thrown down, then held by the throat.

"Enough!" Darren commanded. "Alex, I should kill you, but the punishment you will receive from my disappointed sister will be far worse. I suggest you leave now."

Darren released him. Alex looked angry, but he returned slowly to his place by Chloe's side.

I had a burning hatred for Alex and wanted to kill him. Make him pay for torturing me. He was truly a monster and deserved to die like one.

Darren's concern and warning carried through the air to me. They were strong. He knew how I felt, and wanted to make it clear to me to leave it alone. I understood, but didn't like it.

Darren faced his sister. Her calm exterior had eroded and irritation was evident. "So sister, I believe you owe me an explanation." Darren stepped closer to her. "Why the hell would you do this? Are you insane?"

"My dear brother." She patted his cheek like a child. "You had it coming to you. You destroyed something of mine. It is only fair I return the favour."

Chloe recomposed herself. "I hadn't realized you would have saved this one. I thought for sure you would have played the martyr once again. Another lover lost, another that you could have saved but instead let slip through your fingers. It seems, my dear brother, this one is special. And for that, I will make sure he pays the price if it is the last thing that I do!"

"Try sister." Darren grabbed my hand, turning to me for reassurance. I smiled. He continued. "You can waste your eternity trying, but you will never succeed. I will make sure of that. You come anywhere near Markus, and I will rid you of that waste of flesh that stands by your side. Then I will come for you."

Darren's hand tightened around mine. He meant what he said. I was proud of him. Chloe was at a loss for words.

Out of nowhere someone spoke.

"Uhmm, like, can't we all just be friends?" came the familiar voice of Claire. "I hate it when family argues. We all need to be happy, because there could be worse things you know."

Chloe turned to Claire. "Shut up you useless cow!" Chloe stepped towards the couch where Claire sat. "You have fulfilled your usefulness to me now. I suggest you leave."

Claire held up and shook the little blue book in her hand. "Yes, thanks for this. There are some great spells in here. It will definitely add to my collection."

I stared. I didn't understand. "Claire?" I stepped towards her. "What are you doing here? You helped Chloe? What's going on?"

"Oh Hiya Markus. Well, you see Darren's sister offered me this spell book if I could find you for her. So I did." Claire beamed.

"Why would you do that? I thought you were my friend?" I

couldn't believe that Claire would ever do something like that to me.

"Oh Markus, the funny thing is, the joke is on her. The nasty blood sucker she is." Claire squealed with delight. "Oh it's too good."

Chloe – now fully irritated – barked at her. "What do you mean? What joke? Speak!"

There was a pink flash on the couch. A frumpy old woman in a bright shiny pink leisure suit appeared. She had a wrinkled face, and fuchsia lipstick bleeding into the crevices around the lips.

Shocked, I yelled out. "Marge? What are you doing here?"

Why on earth was my land lady here? It made no sense.

"OY!" She bellowed in her heavy Boston accent, while getting up off the couch. "Whatt, are ya stupid? Can't figure it out?" Marge waved her hand in front of Claire's face. "Sleep." she said. Claire's eyes closed and she immediately started to snore.

"Now." Marge grumped. "Let's get down to business. I haven't gawt all day"

We, the vampires stood staring at her. It was clear none of us had the faintest idea what she wanted.

Marge started again. Her accent became thicker. "So, where is he? Hmm? Tell me." She pointed her finger at Chloe. "You! You know, I know you do. C'mon, give him up."

Chloe stood silent. It was unclear whether she knew who Marge meant or if she was shocked by this horrendous frump demanding something of her.

Marge began to pace back and forth. The light in the room glinted and sparkled off her shiny leisure suit. She was a spectacle. She paused in front of me and looked me up and down.

"Well, this all worked out for you didn't it? I always like for things to go my way." She poked me. "Shame though, you had a little gift, we could have helped it along. Oh well, worth it in the end. That's the price you pay. Now it's gone for good, since you're one of them now."

I was confused. I didn't like the old bag touching me. It sent a chill down my spine. But there was something odd about Marge. And strangely familiar.

"What are you talking about?" I asked. "Marge are you drunk?"

Marge tilted her head back and laughed, actually it was a cackle. "Silly boy. Drunk? Me? I bet I could drink just about anyone under the table. Don't make me laugh. What I'm talking about is you played your part perfectly. From the first day I met you, I knew this would work out just fine. Well, as long as you didn't have to use that pea brain of yours."

Darren stepped forward. "Watch your mouth hag."

"Oh? And what are you going to do about it you soulless monster? C'mon, take your best shot at me."

Again Marge cackled uncontrollably like an escapee from the loony bin.

When she regained herself she spoke to me again. "You haven't figured out who I am yet have you dimwit? I didn't think you were that slow. In over 500 years always the same, pretty face means no brains. Haa Haa haaaa!"

Darren put his hand on my back. His concern and comfort circled around me. He felt I was smart and he would never make me feel dumb.

Marge spoke. She dropped the humour – and her accent. Her voice changed and sounded very different, yet familiar. "Well, boy. Seeing as you will never figure it out, I also have a last name. It's Havish." A pink flash and there stood Ms. Havish, exactly the same as she always had been. "Yes, that's right, it's me boy, the same one who helped you since you were a child. Amazing what a witch can do."

My jaw dropped. Never in a million years would I have thought there was any connection between the two old women. Why was this happening?

Ms. Havish sneered at me. "Do you have any idea how hard it is to find this particular family of vampires? Hmm? Do you?"

I shook my head.

She continued. "Vampires are only possible to find if they allow you to find them. This family of day vampires, well, I have been hunting them for a very long time, and now, finally I've got them. All thanks to you, Markus!"

I looked from Ms. Havish to Darren. "What do I have to do with any of this?"

"Well, boy," she answered. "I could never find them. I had no choice but to seek out the Gypsies. They are a powerful and solitary clan of witches. For a favour it will cost you dearly. However, this was worth it.

They told me of a child with a particular gift. If I found this child, I could nurture him, mould his mind, force his interests the way I wanted and ensure his trust. Did you ever wonder *why* I always fed you vampire books? The gypsies said your gift would call out to the vampires I hunted for, it would bring them to you, enabling me to finally find them."

There was silence. I struggled to hold back tears of hurt. The one person who was always there for me growing up ..."I can't believe you used me."

"Boy, you were helpless and useless. You actually aggravated me more often than not. Every-time I entered your mind to track you, you blacked out. It was annoying. So I used your chubby friend here. Claire is it? It was easy enough to put her under my spell and control her. I got the idea to follow you through that black cat that's always around. But now, even if you are a vampire, I can find *you* Markus. I have been in your mind and would be able to sniff you out."

Darren spoke up. "What do you want with us? Why would you want to find us? Who are you really?"

"What do I want?" She cackled again. "I want to get rid of you all. But first I need you to tell me where your maker is."

Chloe stepped towards Ms. Havish. "What do you want of him? Why should we tell you?"

"Because." Ms. Havish responded. "He owes me. So, tell me where he is or I'm going to get nasty with you all."

Ms. Havish stepped forward and started waving her hand around. She was making circular motions.

Chloe stepped in front of her. "Leave here hag. We will never tell you where he is. You cannot force us." Chloe stood with her hands on her hips.

With a grin on her face, Ms. Havish raised her hands and thrust them forward. A surge of air came from them and hit Chloe. She was thrown backwards with amazing force and tumbled down the staircase.

Alex flung himself at the witch. She flicked her hand and he was swept to the side. Chloe charged up the stairs. She wore an expression of sheer malevolence. Like an angry bull she trampled Ms. Havish. The two women wrestled and rolled. Chloe tried to sink her teeth into her, and Ms. Havish tried desperately to push her off. Chloe had the upper hand as she was physically more powerful. Her fangs were nearing the old witch's neck.

The air blew in the room, flowing directly towards the hag and the vampire. Again, Ms. Havish unleashed a gale that threw Chloe's body against the wall, freeing her to get up.

Alex attacked her. This time Ms. Havish did not fling him off like a mosquito. In a split second a miniature violent tornado caught him as he ran at her. She muttered something inaudible. There was a snapping sound and Alex's body dropped to the floor in a heap. He was twisted and knotted in an impossible mutilation.

Darren grabbed my hand and pulled me backwards. His stress and worry hung over us. He was scared for us.

Chloe got up. She gawked at Alex laying on the floor. He must be dead. Darren and I could see the rage on her face. There was a determination there. She would kill Ms. Havish or be killed trying. She flew at the witch. They smashed together and the struggle began anew.

Darren wasted no time. He lifted me over his shoulder and ran for it.

Ms. Havish screamed out at us. "I *will* find you two. I can *always* find *you* Markus! Then you can tell me where the maker is before I kill the lot of you!"

We were at the front door when Chloe and the witch started to bellow at each other. The air in the street began to pull into the store. It was going to get bad. Darren was at the vehicle and inside in a blink of an eye. Sheer panic was emanating from him. He closed my door and jumped over the hood and got inside. He threw the keys in the ignition and sped away. He grabbed for my hand and squeezed it tightly. Almost to the point that it started to hurt.

We were silent as Darren drove. There was no need for words, our emotions passed between us. There was worry for Chloe, worry for Claire, worry about us and what was going to happen. It was so much to process. I didn't know why Ms. Havish wanted Darren's maker so badly. I wanted to ask him but I didn't think the timing was right.

Instead, I gazed out the window and then to him. He would occasionally glance at me, seeming to read my soul. It calmed me. I thought I was lucky to be here with him.

Hours later, Darren finally spoke.

"Markus, I'm sorry you got involved with all of this. I should have kept my distance in the beginning, and you would have been fine."

"Fine? Are you kidding me? Look how I managed to bring Alex to me. If it wasn't for you, I would have been killed a couple times already."

Darren shook his head. "No, Alex was sent by Chloe. But, I think you are right, maybe you would have still played a part no matter what changed, at least that is what the witch said."

I turned in my seat. "Darren?"

"Yes?"

"Do you think Chloe is alright?" It was a blunt question, but I needed to know.

"I honestly don't know Markus. She is older than I am, and she is very skilled. It seemed Ms. Havish was struggling with her. I think it is safe to assume, Chloe has a fighting chance, or at least a chance to escape."

"Are you worried about her?" I asked.

"Of course, a little, but if it's the end for her, so be it. She tried to kill you to hurt me. So I can accept it if that is the case. We were never close."

I processed what he said. The dark highway stretched and wound before us. Trees flashed past us, there was no light except from the moon and the stars above us in the sky.

I finally caved and forced myself to ask. "Why did Ms. Havish want to know where your maker is? Would something bad happen if she found him?"

"I do not know why she wanted him. But I can assure you Markus, she cannot harm him. No one ever knows where he is, even us. He lets you know when he will see you. We could never have told her where he was."

"Darren, I thought you had parents?" I was confused.

"I do. He is my father and his mate is my mother."

"Your own dad doesn't tell you where to find him?" I found that a bit shocking, more so than the fact Darren's parents were vampires.

"As I told you, we prearrange our meetings." Darren explained. "If I don't show up, then I wait for a message from him and my mother for the next opportunity."

"That just sounds confusing. So, he made you a vampire?"

"Yes. They both did. He and my mother."

Both? Maybe that was a typical thing. I would ask about that later. "If Ms. Havish ever did find them, could anything happen to you?" I asked.

Darren grinned. "It's not like in the books or movies Markus. If they die, I will still be here holding your hand. And we will still be vampires."

I sighed. " Well that's a relief. I was scared ... you know."

"Yes, I know."

Darren pulled off the road into a empty parking lot. We stopped at what appeared to be a strip mall. The lights were dimmed and the entire place was deserted. It was too late at night for it to be open. He drove around the back of the building.

He stopped and turned the ignition off. We got out and stretched. It was the first time I noticed new sounds, I mean *really* noticed them. I could hear the rodents digging in the dumpster. The raccoons climbing in the trees overhead. It wasn't just that. I could smell them too. They all had their own very distinct scent. It was amazing I never noticed that when I was human. I stood in awe of how different things were.

Darren motioned to me. He walked to the back door of the mall. When we reached it he easily pulled it right off the hinges. He set it down beside the entrance way. I decided to give it a shot and try to lift the heavy metal door myself. I could do it, but it took an enormous amount of effort. It was safe to assume that Darren was much stronger.

Darren spoke. "Strength, agility, speed, all those skills get better and stronger with time Markus. So please don't fret. Just think, in a hundred years we will be laughing at you for breaking a sweat trying to lift a door."

I blushed. Sweat beaded on my forehead. I wiped. Pinkish water. Was it supposed to look like that?

Darren patted me on the back, and we moved on further into the store.

It was dim inside, only a few security spot lights were on. It didn't make any difference to me. I could make out where I was going. I realized I had vision similar to night vision goggles. Anything that was in darkness was clear, but in muted colours. I was starting to wonder what else would be different.

Darren stopped in the men's department of the store we were in. He called to me and pointed to his right. "Pick out a new shirt and jeans. The rack right over there."

He began to rifle through the underware and t-shirts.

I found a pair of dark blue jeans and a red t-shirt with a union jack printed on it. I thought it looked fun. I went to Darren and showed him.

"Is this alright?" I wasn't completely sure what occasion I was dressing for.

"Yes, that will do. Now, take off all your clothes. We need to change and then leave." Darren started to undress. "Even those, Markus." He smirked as he snapped the waistband of my boxers.

"Uhmm, why? I just put these on his morning." I asked, more from feeling a little self conscious. I was also getting aroused at the prospect of seeing Darren naked.

"Markus. We need to get out of these clothes. If that witch is following us she can probably track us by scent too. She made mention of sniffing you out, so I'm not taking any chances. Besides, she knows what we smell like, as well as Chloe and Alex, and we have their scents all over our clothes. So if we get rid of it, the scent will change slighty, it might be enough to throw her off our track a little. Maybe give us a little extra time."

"She can smell like we do?" I had never read about witches having abilities like that.

"Who knows? But I'm sure she can probably control some creature that can."

Now I was worried.

Darren had his shirt off and his pants were in a heap on the floor. My worry vanished as I surveyed his perfect body. It was impossible not to notice. I could see every ripple, every muscle, the close-cropped hair on his chest, the hair that lead down ...

Darren pulled off his underwear.

My jaw must have dropped, I wasn't sure. I had never seen someone so perfect. I felt myself becoming erect, and saw Darren was reacting the same.

He stepped forward and came to me. I felt his hands on my bare arms. He slid them up my shoulders and then down my chest. I held my breath, it was so intense. I had never had someone touch me like this before.

Darren grabbed me and pulled me in close. He forced my mouth open with his tongue and kissed me. My body melted, yet I was so aroused, heated and impassioned with excitement. We wrapped our arms around each other and roughly grabbed and kneaded each other's skin.

We dropped to the floor, Darren forced himself on top of me. He began to caress and kiss my skin. I wanted him so badly, and he knew it. He worked his way up to my throat, he kissed and licked. Suddenly Darren sunk his fangs into me.

My body spasmed. It was not pain, it was pure ecstasy. The feel of him tasting me was intense. A euphoric climax. He stopped, grinning widely. It was clear he was loving every minute of it. I leaned up – my fangs protruded – he lowered his neck just enough for me to bite into him.

Again, the rush. This time it was followed by a new sensation. No words will ever describe how it felt. Darren entered my body, and thrust hard. Intense passion filled me inside. Frenzied, I thirsted for more and continued to drink from him. I wanted this to last forever.

CHAPTER TEN
THE BEGINNING

Darren and I were seated in the car. We were both quiet – there was no need for words at the moment. Instead, he drove us back onto the highway. We went back to his house. Darren went inside and grabbed some necessities. I waited in the vehicle. He said it was for my safety.

Darren was on alert. Apparently, someone or something had already been here. His things had be riffled through, and the furniture had been tossed around. There was no new scent left, so there was no telling what managed this.

I rested my head back on the seat as we drove. The darkness outside would end soon and the sun would be rising. I opened my window a crack to let in some fresh air. The smell of the ocean miles away carried on the spring breeze. I put my window down more and breathed deeply.

THUD.

Something hit the car. We swerved, Darren pulled at the wheel to steady the car back onto the road again. He must have hit something big. Funny we didn't see it.

THUD.

We were bashed from my side and Darren swerved onto the shoulder of the road.

Sitting straight up, I spun my head around, trying to see what it was. There was nothing.

THUD.

The car was slammed again and forcing it to swerve. Darren put his foot all the way down on the gas peddle. This attack was not natural. He kept glancing at the rear view mirror. The road started to bend and wind, we were going down hill.

Faster and faster we drove. I wasn't sure how Darren could handle the car at this speed. Everything was flashing by. Even with my new vampire skills, I couldn't keep up with it.

The trees were beginning to thin, the salty smell of the ocean was stronger. The sky ahead was starting to lighten, morning was coming. And then I could finally see the ocean in front of us. We were driving towards it. Darren's emotions carried a sense of relief and yet urgency. We must be close to where he wanted to go.

A loud screeching filled the silence.

The back window of the car shattered into a million pieces. It was hit hard, but even as I turned to look, I still couldn't see what did it. The broken window was suddenly torn out and flung backwards onto the road.

The loud screeching sound came again, this time it was close. Very close.

Darren stared out the front of the vehicle. He didn't bother looking back anymore. Both his hands gripped tightly to the steering wheel, as he drove as fast as he could. My panic mixed with his own. He was trying to save our lives.

The screeching continued. There were no breaks in it anymore. Its pitch went up and down, almost as if it was a form of speech. What ever it was, it was fast. Too fast for us to see it, and so fast it could keep up with our car.

The car was slammed from the back. We lurched forward. It came again, this time from above. The roof caved slightly. I ducked down and covered my head with my arms, shielding myself from it.

BOOM, BOOM. The sides of the vehicle were hit by the unknown thing. It was slowly crushing the car in from all sides. We were going to be crushed to death.

The front windshield smashed outwards from the pressure. Darren jerked the wheel from being startled. I cried out. This was the end.

"Oh my god, Darren. We're going to DIE!" I was terror stricken.

"No we are NOT!" Darren shouted at me.

He turned the car dramatically. We went so fast that only two wheels were touching the pavement. Darren steadied us again and then slammed his foot down on the gas peddle. I was slammed back into my seat.

Darren reached over and released my seat belt and then his own. He looked at me and forced a smile. "I will not let anything bad ever happen to you, Markus."

I had no time to reply. We slammed into something solid and were thrown out the front of the vehicle with such force. It was happening too quickly to see. I slammed into a hard surface and rebounded. I rolled and scraped, my skin was getting slashed and spiked with hundreds of slivers. Again, I bashed into something and then fell downwards.

It felt like I was falling forever, but I hit ice cold wetness. I plunged to the bottom of the ocean floor. I opened my eyes. It was impossible to focus in this murky darkness. The slimy plants swished and flicked around me. I struggled to swim to the surface, but the current was too strong. Again I tried. My body was pulled back and further out into the depths. I grabbed madly at anything that could steady me.

A hand thrust in front of my face. It caught a hold of me and jerked me up. I reached the surface of the water and was sprayed by the cold mist of the torrent waves.

Darren was beside me. He held onto me by my arm and started to swim us further out into the water. He was powerful enough that the water posed no threat to him. There was light breaking across the sky, like pink lightning. The sun was rising ahead of us.

A dark cloud shadowed over us. It swirled and flickered angrily. Screeching, it came closer towards the surface of the water. Two vicious talons snapped down to grab hold of us. We froze with dread.

The first sliver of the sun rose above the water, its light cast across us. The cloud faltered and retreated backwards into the darkness behind. It finally disappeared.

We were treading water. Both unsure of what just happened. Darren broke free of his shock and yelled for me to swim.

We swam towards what looked like a large boat in the distance.

It turned out to be a freighter ship. What it carried, I don't know, but we climbed up the high sides and snuck aboard as the inhabitants were all still asleep. We went through a door and found a place to hide amongst the wrapped cargo. Darren wiped the side of my face.

"Are you okay, Markus?" He asked. Concern in his voice.

"Yes ... I just don't understand what happened. What was that thing?"

We sat down and he pulled me close to him, wrapping his arms around me. "I don't know Markus. I have a feeling it has to do with Ms. Havish trying to find us. We need to get far away from here. As far as we can go."

"Okay, you don't have to tell me twice." I lay my head on his chest, it felt safe. "I'm so tired. This has been a very long day, or night. Whatever you want to call it."

"A very long rising you mean."

"What?"

"That's what we call it when you are turned. Rising. I have never known any vampire who has gone through what you have on the first day of their rising."

"Oh, well, go figure. I always seem to get the short end of the stick, don't I? Can nothing good ever happen to me?"

Darren frowned. The sadness rippled from him.

"What's wrong?" I asked.

"Nothing Markus. I just thought ... you know ..." The sadness changed to nervousness. He took a breath and continued. "I thought we had a special moment, you know, I thought we were both happy, together, even if it was only for that time."

"OHHHH." I smacked my forehead with my hand. "Yes. Of course we did Darren. I'm sorry. I'm just feeling sorry for myself, I didn't mean to upset you. Yes, that was the best thing that has happened in my whole life."

He whispered. "Really?"

"Yes." I lifted up to kiss him softly. "So, now what are we going to do?"

"First things first." Darren said, sounding more confident. "We take this boat to where ever it's going and then find a way to Europe. There are a lot of places we can hide. And we need to find out what that thing was, and how to stop it – and stop Ms. Havish."

"Do you think your parents might know, Darren?"

"Maybe. Maybe we should look for them and ask."

"Well, at least we have a plan." I was relieved. "But what about money or food?"

Darren laughed. "Markus, I have plenty of money stashed away all around the world, so please don't worry. As for food, I will teach you to hunt." He grinned. "But for now, I don't mind if you bite me."

I raised my eyebrow. I knew I should be worried about what was chasing us, and we did need to find out how to stop Ms. Havish. But I was sure we would be okay for now. While the sun shone, we were safe from that thing. Besides. I was hungry – and Darren was too good to pass up.